BILLY BATSON
AND THE MAGIC OF
SHAZAM!

STONE ARCH BOOKS
a capstone imprint

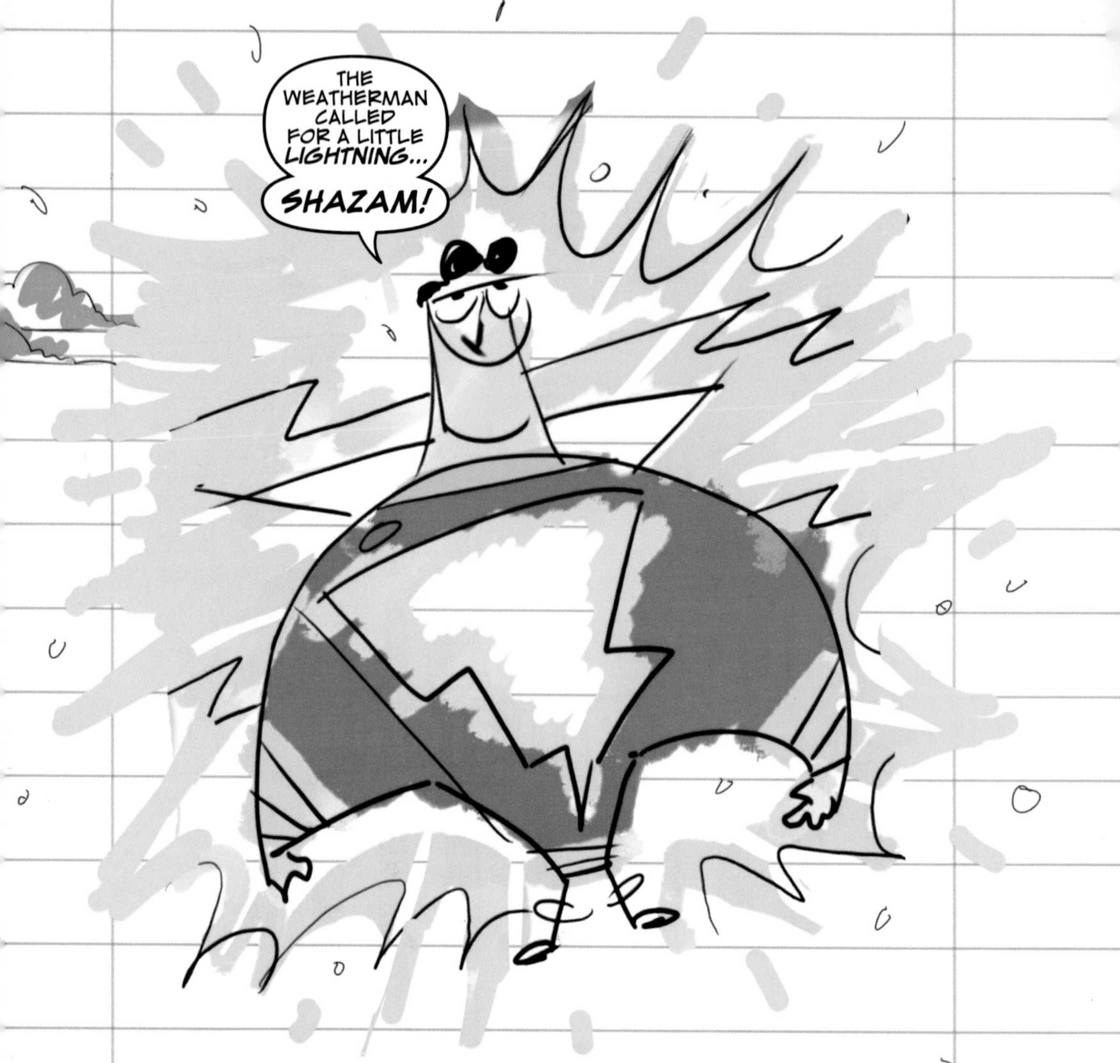
THE WEATHERMAN CALLED FOR A LITTLE LIGHTNING...
SHAZAM!

STONE ARCH BOOKS™

Published in 2015 by Stone Arch Books
A Capstone Imprint
1710 Roe Crest Drive
North Mankato, MN 56003
www.capstonepub.com

Originally published by DC Comics in the U.S.
in single magazine form as Billy Batson and
the Magic of SHAZAM! #10.

DC COMICS
1700 Broadway, New York, NY 10019
A Warner Bros. Entertainment Company

Printed in China by Nordica.
0914/CA21401510
092014 008470NORDS15

Cataloging-in-Publication Data is available at the Library
of Congress website.
ISBN: 978-1-4342-9746-4 (library binding)

Summary: As Captain Marvel struggles to keep his superpowers under control, a new and dangerous enemy takes Mary Marvel out of the picture. Will our favorite super hero be able to succeed all on his own?

STONE ARCH BOOKS
Ashley C. Andersen Zantop **Publisher**
Michael Dahl **Editorial Director**
Sean Tulien **Editor**
Heather Kindseth **Creative Director**
Kristi Carlson and Peggie Carley **Designers**

DC COMICS
Dan Didio **Original U.S. Editor**

BILLY BATSON AND THE MAGIC OF SHAZAM!

The Legacy of Mr. Banjo!

Art Baltazar & Franco ....writers
Byron Vaughns..........................illustrator
Dave Tanguay............................. colorist

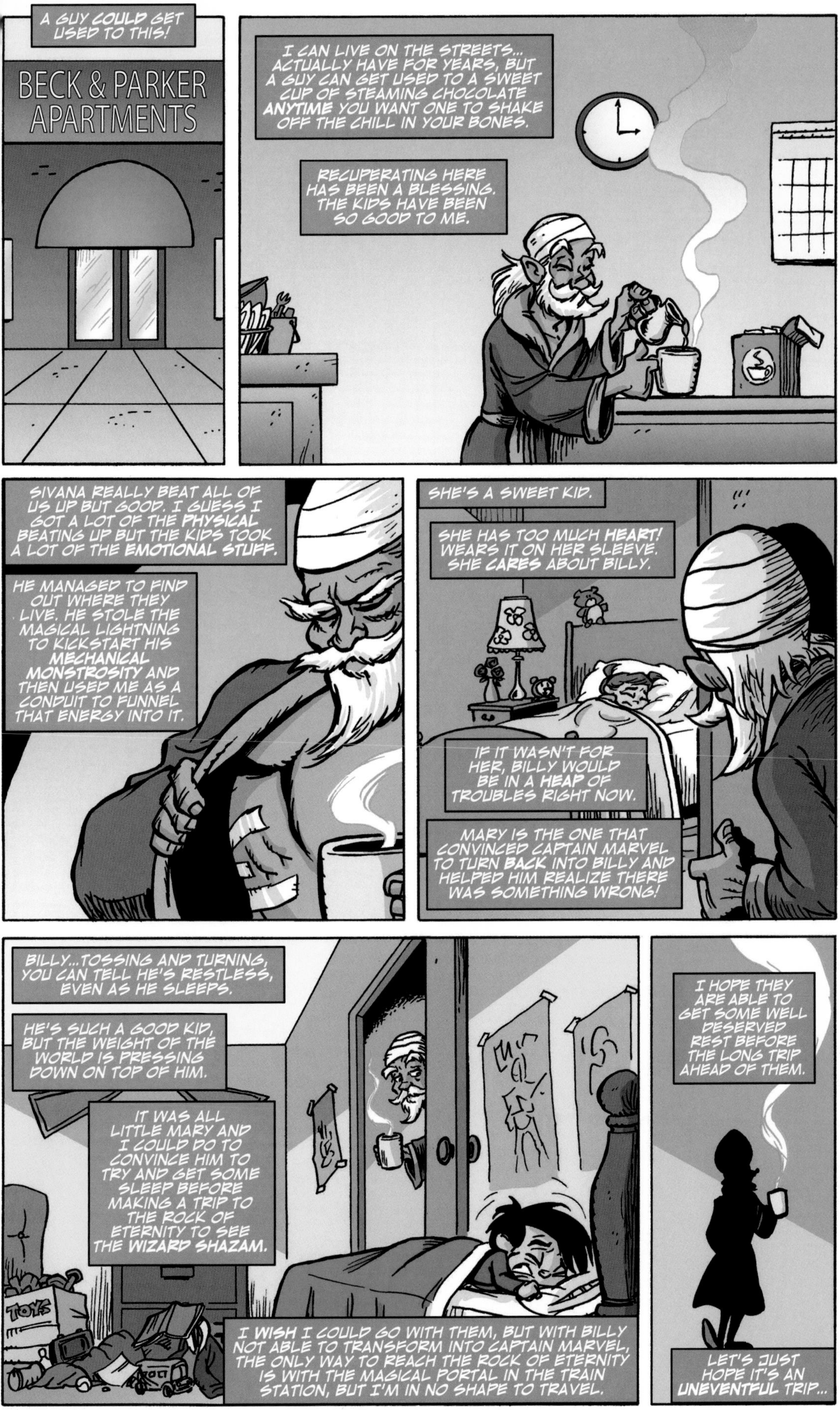
A GUY COULD GET USED TO THIS!
BECK & PARKER APARTMENTS
I CAN LIVE ON THE STREETS... ACTUALLY HAVE FOR YEARS, BUT A GUY CAN GET USED TO A SWEET CUP OF STEAMING CHOCOLATE ANYTIME YOU WANT ONE TO SHAKE OFF THE CHILL IN YOUR BONES.
RECUPERATING HERE HAS BEEN A BLESSING. THE KIDS HAVE BEEN SO GOOD TO ME.
SIVANA REALLY BEAT ALL OF US UP BUT GOOD. I GUESS I GOT A LOT OF THE PHYSICAL BEATING UP BUT THE KIDS TOOK A LOT OF THE EMOTIONAL STUFF.
HE MANAGED TO FIND OUT WHERE THEY LIVE. HE STOLE THE MAGICAL LIGHTNING TO KICKSTART HIS MECHANICAL MONSTROSITY AND THEN USED ME AS A CONDUIT TO FUNNEL THAT ENERGY INTO IT.
SHE'S A SWEET KID.
SHE HAS TOO MUCH HEART! WEARS IT ON HER SLEEVE. SHE CARES ABOUT BILLY.
IF IT WASN'T FOR HER, BILLY WOULD BE IN A HEAP OF TROUBLES RIGHT NOW.
MARY IS THE ONE THAT CONVINCED CAPTAIN MARVEL TO TURN BACK INTO BILLY AND HELPED HIM REALIZE THERE WAS SOMETHING WRONG!
BILLY...TOSSING AND TURNING, YOU CAN TELL HE'S RESTLESS, EVEN AS HE SLEEPS.
HE'S SUCH A GOOD KID, BUT THE WEIGHT OF THE WORLD IS PRESSING DOWN ON TOP OF HIM.
IT WAS ALL LITTLE MARY AND I COULD DO TO CONVINCE HIM TO TRY AND GET SOME SLEEP BEFORE MAKING A TRIP TO THE ROCK OF ETERNITY TO SEE THE WIZARD SHAZAM.
TOYS
I WISH I COULD GO WITH THEM, BUT WITH BILLY NOT ABLE TO TRANSFORM INTO CAPTAIN MARVEL, THE ONLY WAY TO REACH THE ROCK OF ETERNITY IS WITH THE MAGICAL PORTAL IN THE TRAIN STATION, BUT I'M IN NO SHAPE TO TRAVEL.
I HOPE THEY ARE ABLE TO GET SOME WELL DESERVED REST BEFORE THE LONG TRIP AHEAD OF THEM.
LET'S JUST HOPE IT'S AN UNEVENTFUL TRIP...

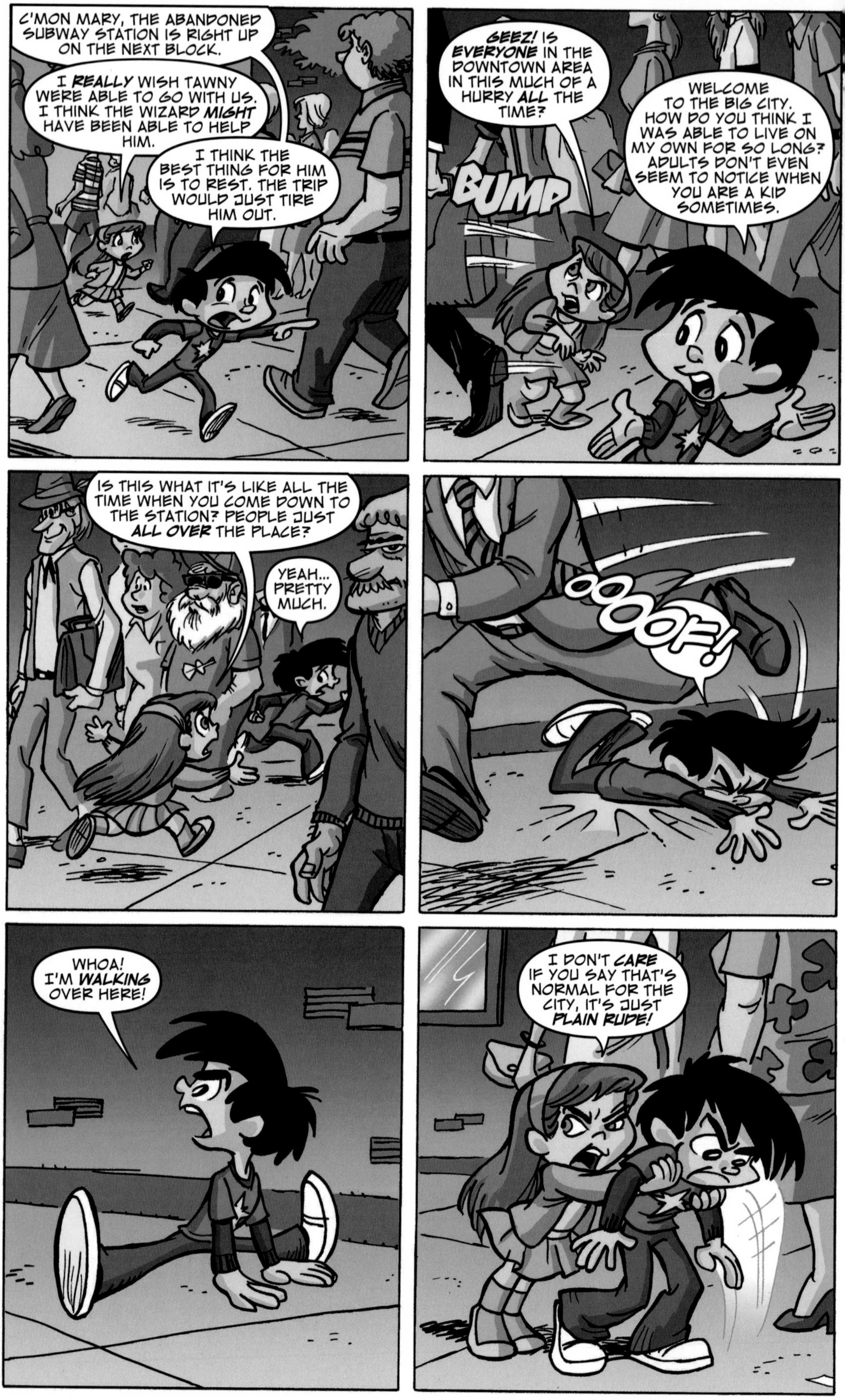
C'MON MARY, THE ABANDONED SUBWAY STATION IS RIGHT UP ON THE NEXT BLOCK.
I REALLY WISH TAWNY WERE ABLE TO GO WITH US. I THINK THE WIZARD MIGHT HAVE BEEN ABLE TO HELP HIM.
I THINK THE BEST THING FOR HIM IS TO REST. THE TRIP WOULD JUST TIRE HIM OUT.
GEEZ! IS EVERYONE IN THE DOWNTOWN AREA IN THIS MUCH OF A HURRY ALL THE TIME?
BUMP
WELCOME TO THE BIG CITY. HOW DO YOU THINK I WAS ABLE TO LIVE ON MY OWN FOR SO LONG? ADULTS DON'T EVEN SEEM TO NOTICE WHEN YOU ARE A KID SOMETIMES.
IS THIS WHAT IT'S LIKE ALL THE TIME WHEN YOU COME DOWN TO THE STATION? PEOPLE JUST ALL OVER THE PLACE?
YEAH... PRETTY MUCH.
OOOOF!
WHOA! I'M WALKING OVER HERE!
I DON'T CARE IF YOU SAY THAT'S NORMAL FOR THE CITY, IT'S JUST PLAIN RUDE!

WELL, *USUALLY* WHEN THEY RUN YOU OVER THEY'RE A BIT MORE *POLITE* THAN THAT.

HEY! DO YOU NOTICE SOMETHING *WEIRD*?

EVERY TIME I COME DOWN *HERE I NOTICE SOMETHING WEIRD.* GIANT ROBOTS, EVEN BIGGER, MORE GIANTER MONSTERS FROM ANOTHER DIMENSION...

WAIT...IS *"GIANTER"* EVEN A WORD?

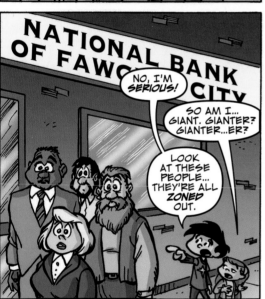

NATIONAL BANK OF FAWCETT CITY

NO, I'M SERIOUS!

SO AM I... GIANT. GIANTER? GIANTER...ER?

LOOK AT THESE PEOPLE... THEY'RE ALL *ZONED* OUT.

YEAH, YOU'RE RIGHT! IT'S LIKE THEY'RE ALL *ZOMBIFIED!* IS THIS WHAT YOU BECOME WHEN YOU'RE AN ADULT AND THEY SAY YOU BECOME A *SLAVE* TO YOUR JOB?

WHERE ARE THEY ALL GOING?

THEY'RE ALL GOING INTO THE *BANK.*

SO WHAT? PEOPLE GO TO THE BANK ALL THE TIME! *WE* NEED TO GET TO THE SUBWAY STATION TO GET TO THE ROCK OF ETERNITY.

NO, THIS IS DIFFERENT! IT'S LIKE THEY'RE *UNDER* A SPELL OR SOMETHING... *C'MON,* WE SHOULD LOOK INTO THIS.

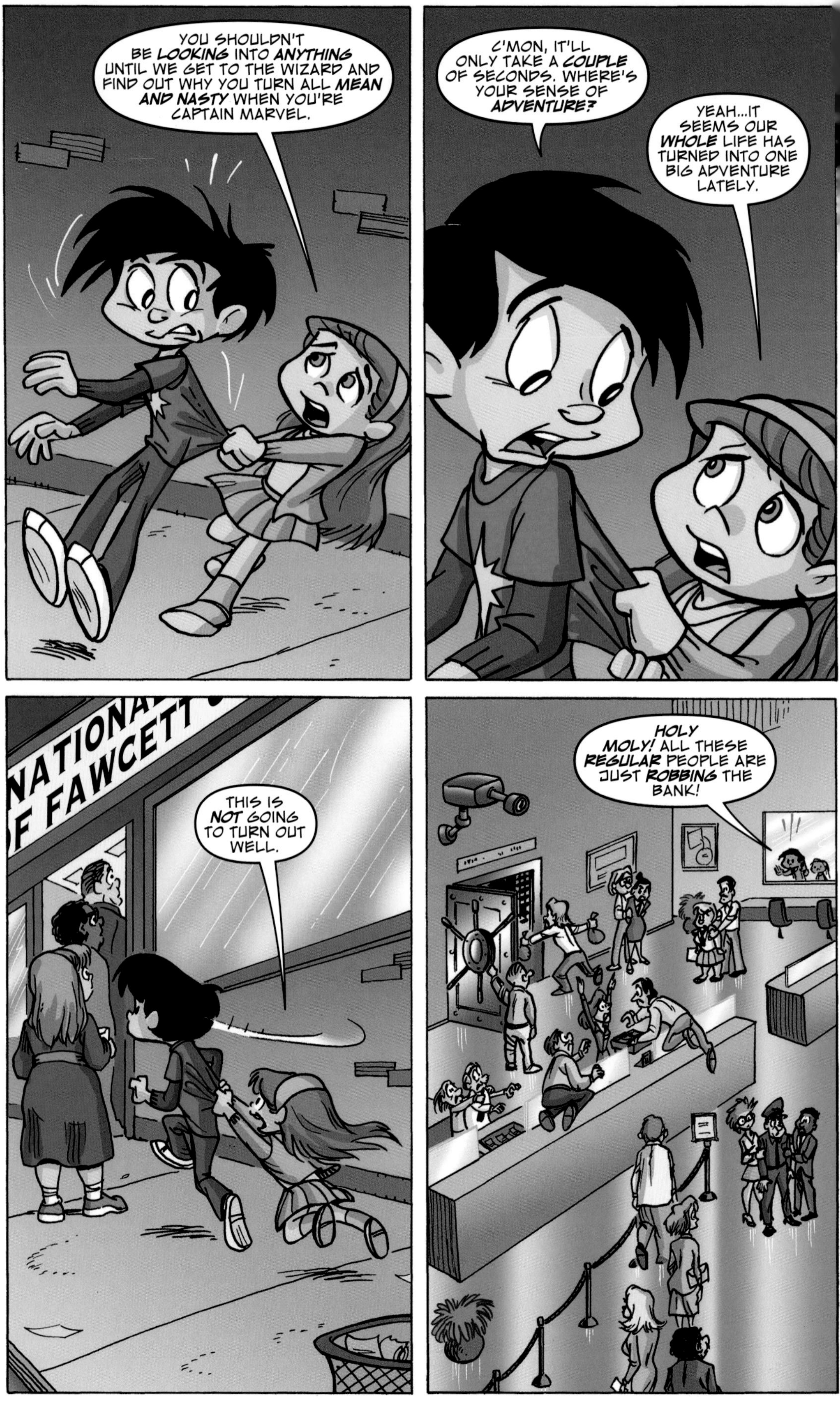
YOU SHOULDN'T BE LOOKING INTO ANYTHING UNTIL WE GET TO THE WIZARD AND FIND OUT WHY YOU TURN ALL MEAN AND NASTY WHEN YOU'RE CAPTAIN MARVEL.
C'MON, IT'LL ONLY TAKE A COUPLE OF SECONDS. WHERE'S YOUR SENSE OF ADVENTURE?
YEAH...IT SEEMS OUR WHOLE LIFE HAS TURNED INTO ONE BIG ADVENTURE LATELY.
NATIONAL
OF FAWCETT
THIS IS NOT GOING TO TURN OUT WELL.
HOLY MOLY! ALL THESE REGULAR PEOPLE ARE JUST ROBBING THE BANK!

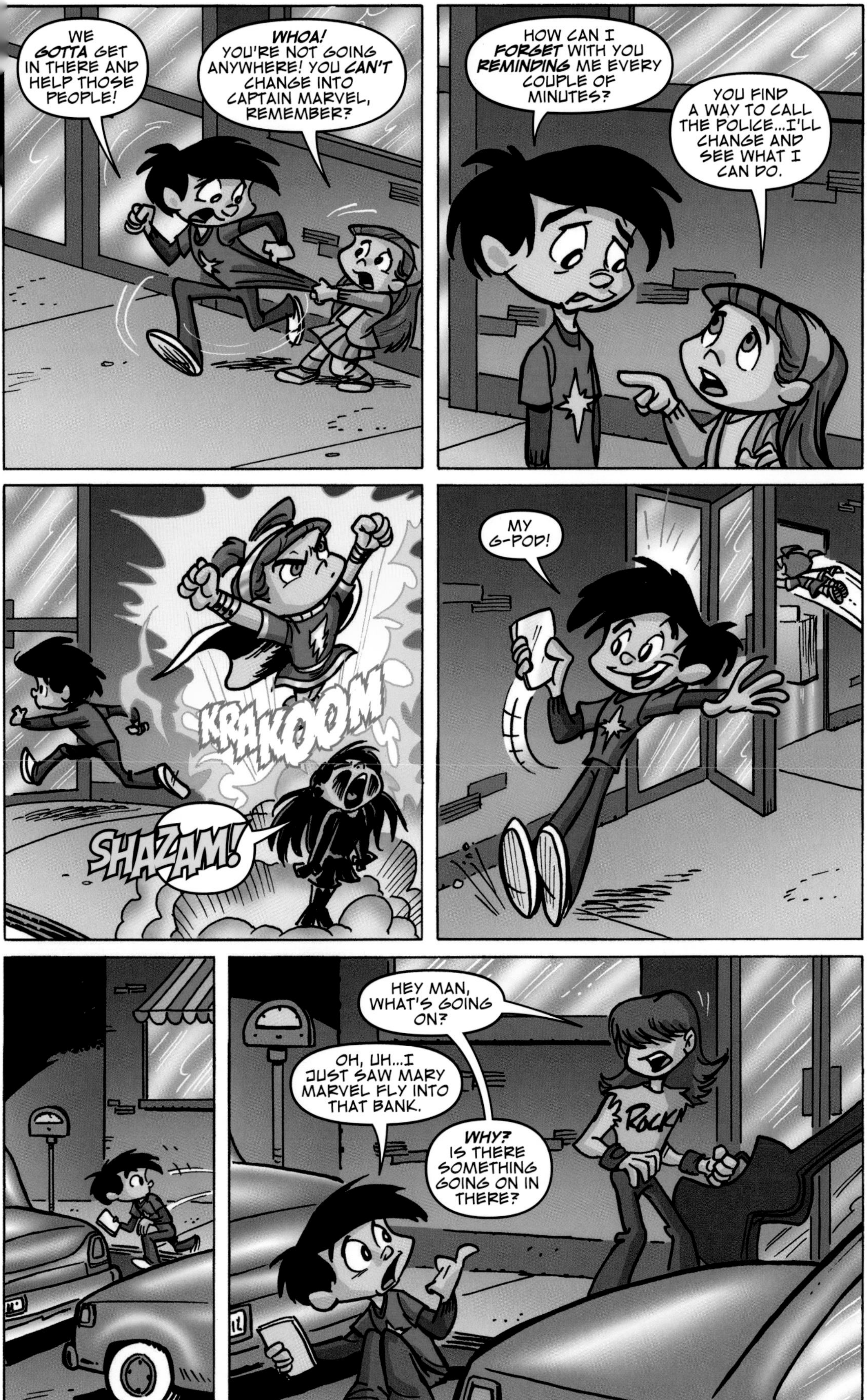
WE GOTTA GET IN THERE AND HELP THOSE PEOPLE!
WHOA! YOU'RE NOT GOING ANYWHERE! YOU CAN'T CHANGE INTO CAPTAIN MARVEL, REMEMBER?
HOW CAN I FORGET WITH YOU REMINDING ME EVERY COUPLE OF MINUTES?
YOU FIND A WAY TO CALL THE POLICE...I'LL CHANGE AND SEE WHAT I CAN DO.
KRAKOOM
SHAZAM!
MY G-POD!
HEY MAN, WHAT'S GOING ON?
OH, UH...I JUST SAW MARY MARVEL FLY INTO THAT BANK.
WHY? IS THERE SOMETHING GOING ON IN THERE?
ROCK

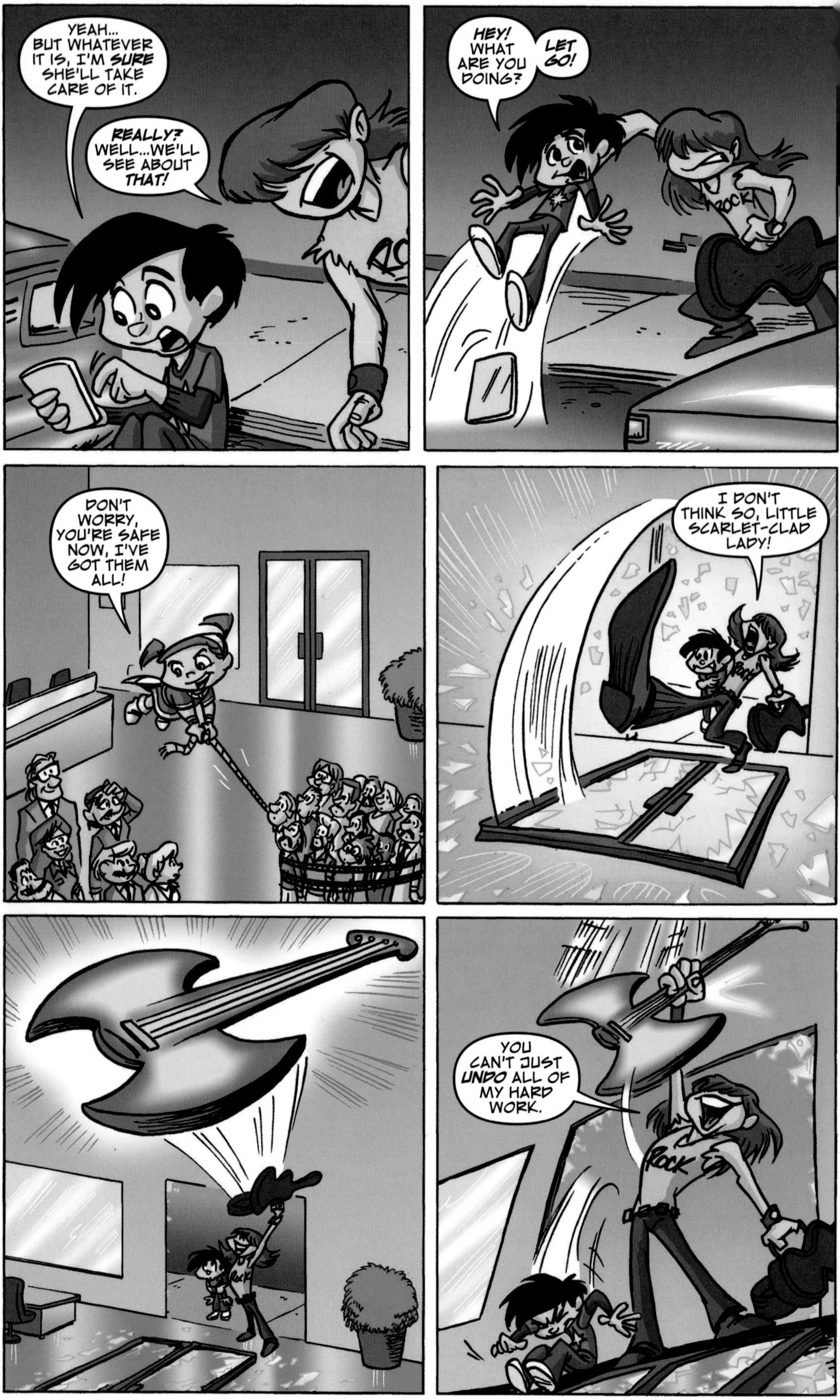
YEAH... BUT WHATEVER IT IS, I'M SURE SHE'LL TAKE CARE OF IT.
REALLY? WELL...WE'LL SEE ABOUT THAT!
HEY! WHAT ARE YOU DOING?
LET GO!
DON'T WORRY, YOU'RE SAFE NOW, I'VE GOT THEM ALL!
I DON'T THINK SO, LITTLE SCARLET-CLAD LADY!
YOU CAN'T JUST UNDO ALL OF MY HARD WORK.

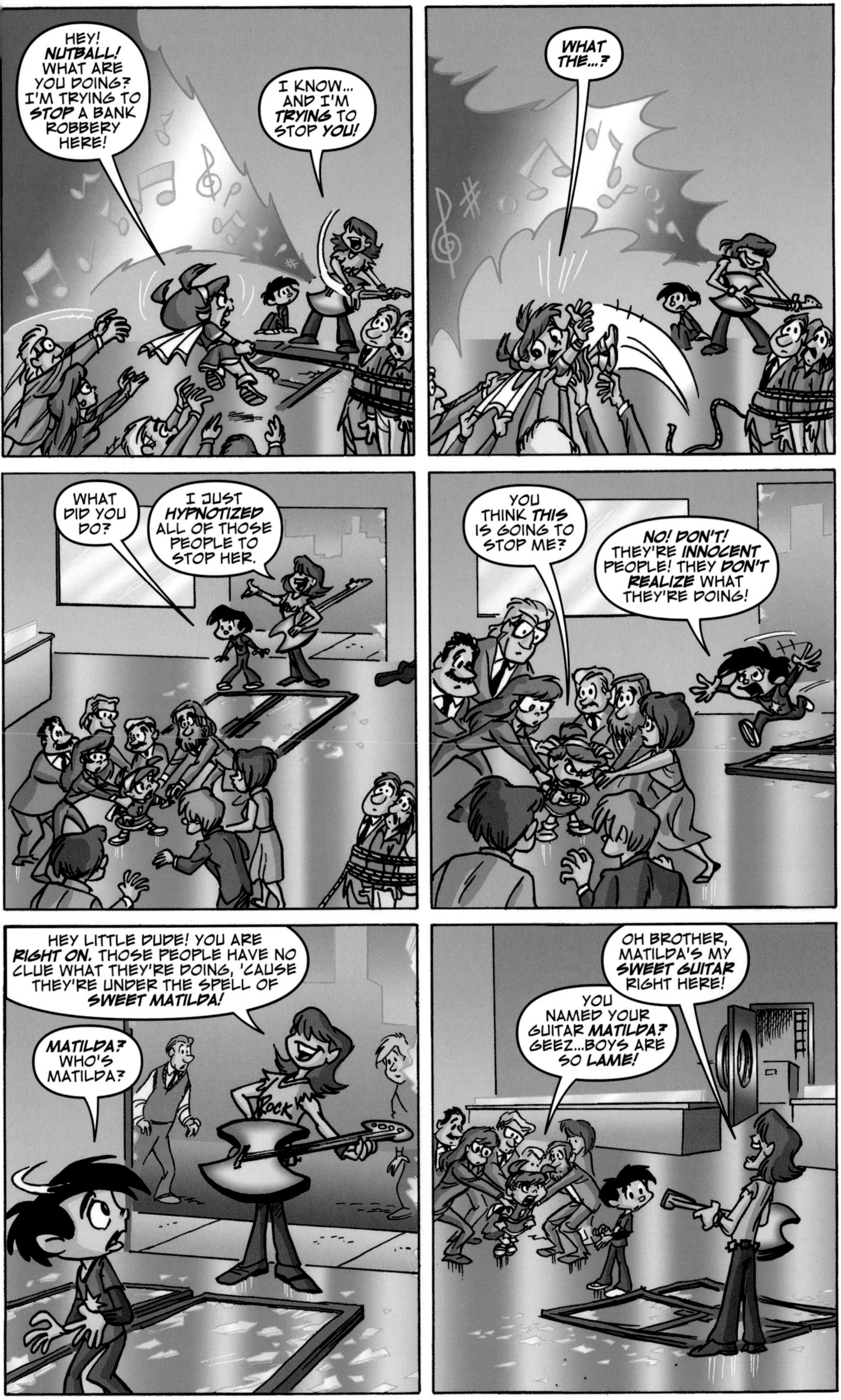
HEY! NUTBALL! WHAT ARE YOU DOING? I'M TRYING TO STOP A BANK ROBBERY HERE!
I KNOW... AND I'M TRYING TO STOP YOU!
WHAT THE...?
WHAT DID YOU DO?
I JUST HYPNOTIZED ALL OF THOSE PEOPLE TO STOP HER.
YOU THINK THIS IS GOING TO STOP ME?
NO! DON'T! THEY'RE INNOCENT PEOPLE! THEY DON'T REALIZE WHAT THEY'RE DOING!
HEY LITTLE DUDE! YOU ARE RIGHT ON. THOSE PEOPLE HAVE NO CLUE WHAT THEY'RE DOING, 'CAUSE THEY'RE UNDER THE SPELL OF SWEET MATILDA!
MATILDA? WHO'S MATILDA?
ROCK
OH BROTHER, MATILDA'S MY SWEET GUITAR RIGHT HERE!
YOU NAMED YOUR GUITAR MATILDA? GEEZ...BOYS ARE SO LAME!

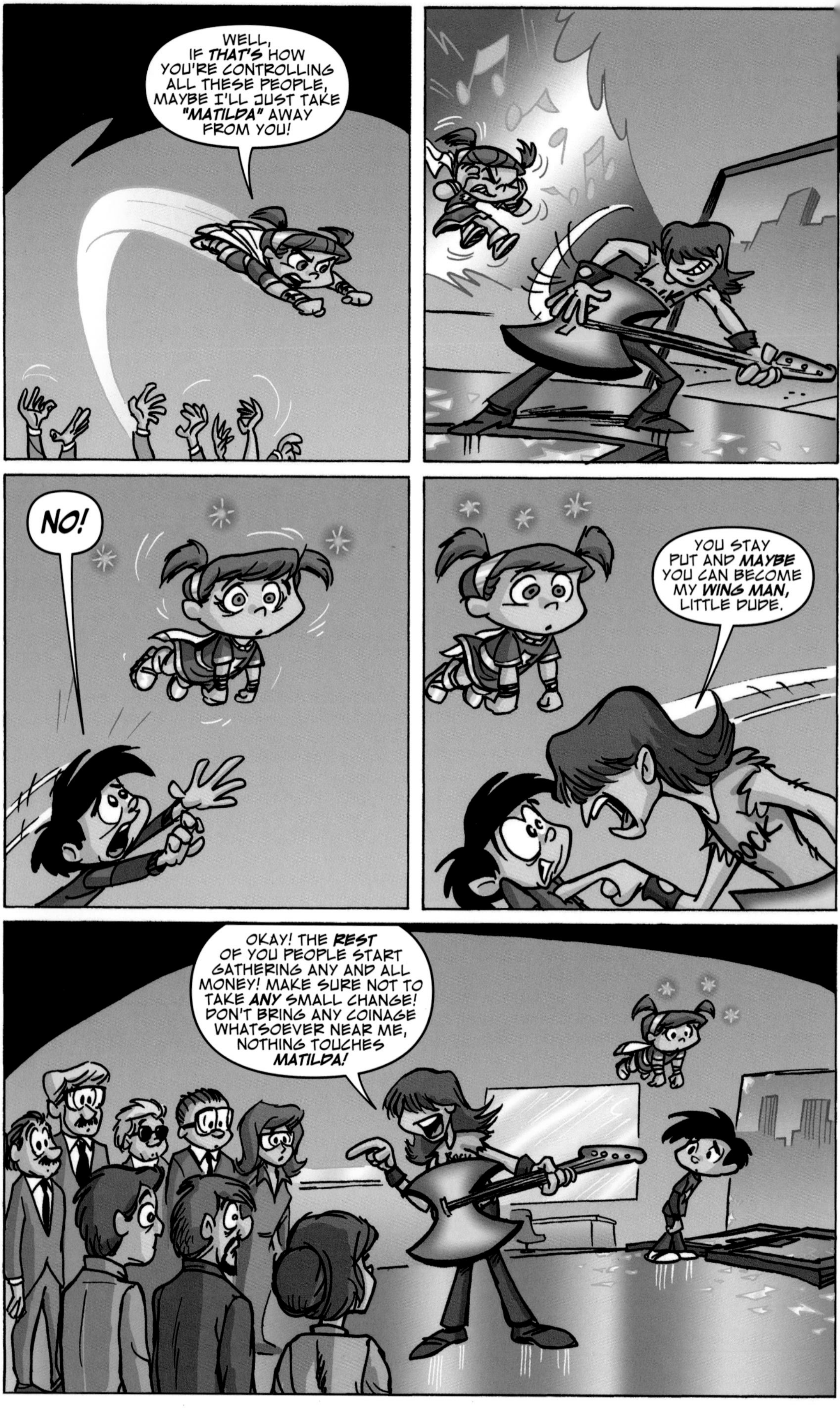
WELL, IF THAT'S HOW YOU'RE CONTROLLING ALL THESE PEOPLE, MAYBE I'LL JUST TAKE "MATILDA" AWAY FROM YOU!
NO!
YOU STAY PUT AND MAYBE YOU CAN BECOME MY WING MAN, LITTLE DUDE.
OKAY! THE REST OF YOU PEOPLE START GATHERING ANY AND ALL MONEY! MAKE SURE NOT TO TAKE ANY SMALL CHANGE! DON'T BRING ANY COINAGE WHATSOEVER NEAR ME, NOTHING TOUCHES MATILDA!

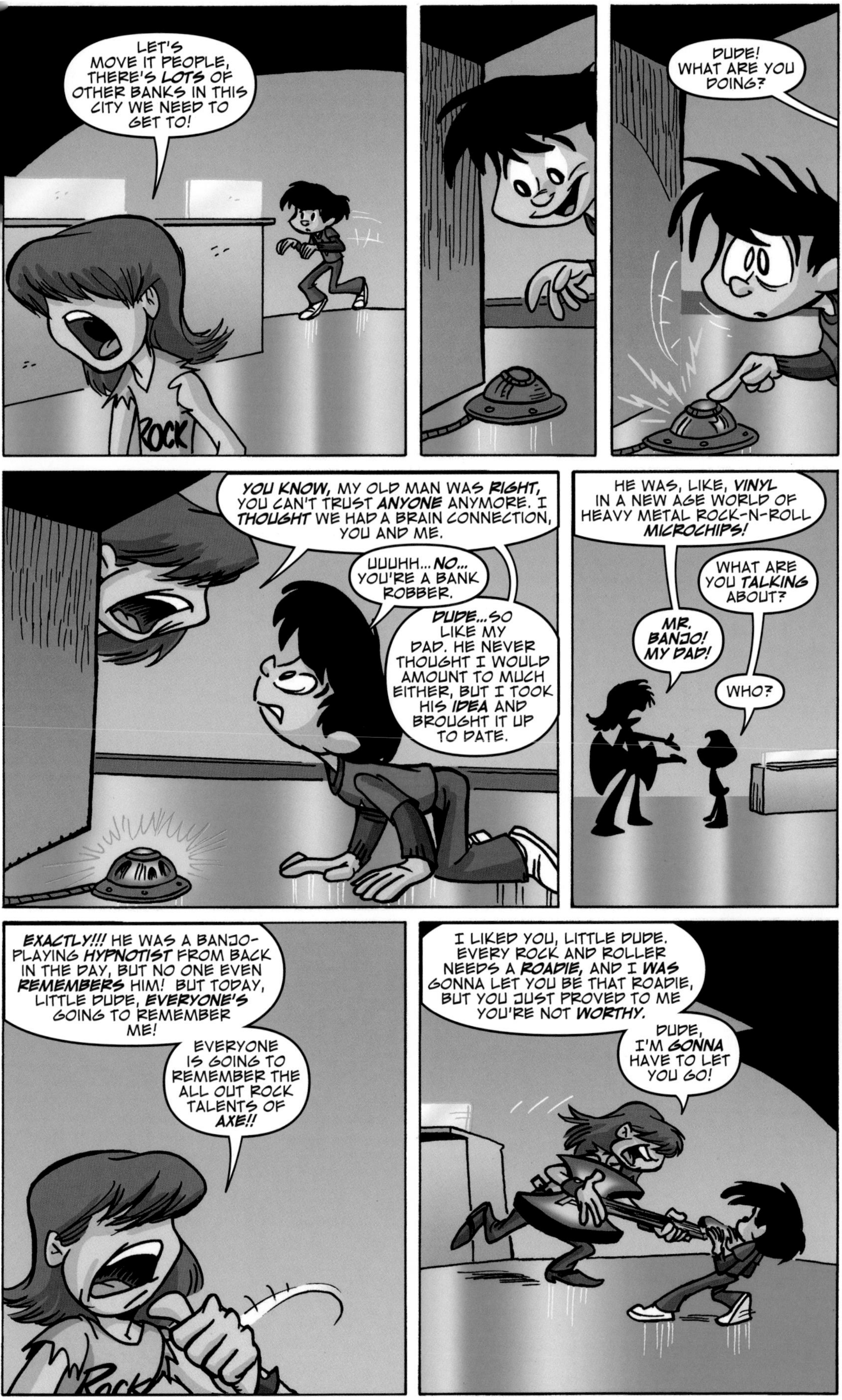
LET'S MOVE IT PEOPLE, THERE'S LOTS OF OTHER BANKS IN THIS CITY WE NEED TO GET TO!
ROCK
DUDE! WHAT ARE YOU DOING?
YOU KNOW, MY OLD MAN WAS RIGHT, YOU CAN'T TRUST ANYONE ANYMORE. I THOUGHT WE HAD A BRAIN CONNECTION, YOU AND ME.
UUUHH... NO... YOU'RE A BANK ROBBER.
DUDE... SO LIKE MY DAD. HE NEVER THOUGHT I WOULD AMOUNT TO MUCH EITHER, BUT I TOOK HIS IDEA AND BROUGHT IT UP TO DATE.
HE WAS, LIKE, VINYL IN A NEW AGE WORLD OF HEAVY METAL ROCK-N-ROLL MICROCHIPS!
WHAT ARE YOU TALKING ABOUT?
MR. BANJO! MY DAD!
WHO?
EXACTLY!!! HE WAS A BANJO-PLAYING HYPNOTIST FROM BACK IN THE DAY, BUT NO ONE EVEN REMEMBERS HIM! BUT TODAY, LITTLE DUDE, EVERYONE'S GOING TO REMEMBER ME!
EVERYONE IS GOING TO REMEMBER THE ALL OUT ROCK TALENTS OF AXE!!
ROCK
I LIKED YOU, LITTLE DUDE. EVERY ROCK AND ROLLER NEEDS A ROADIE, AND I WAS GONNA LET YOU BE THAT ROADIE, BUT YOU JUST PROVED TO ME YOU'RE NOT WORTHY.
DUDE, I'M GONNA HAVE TO LET YOU GO!

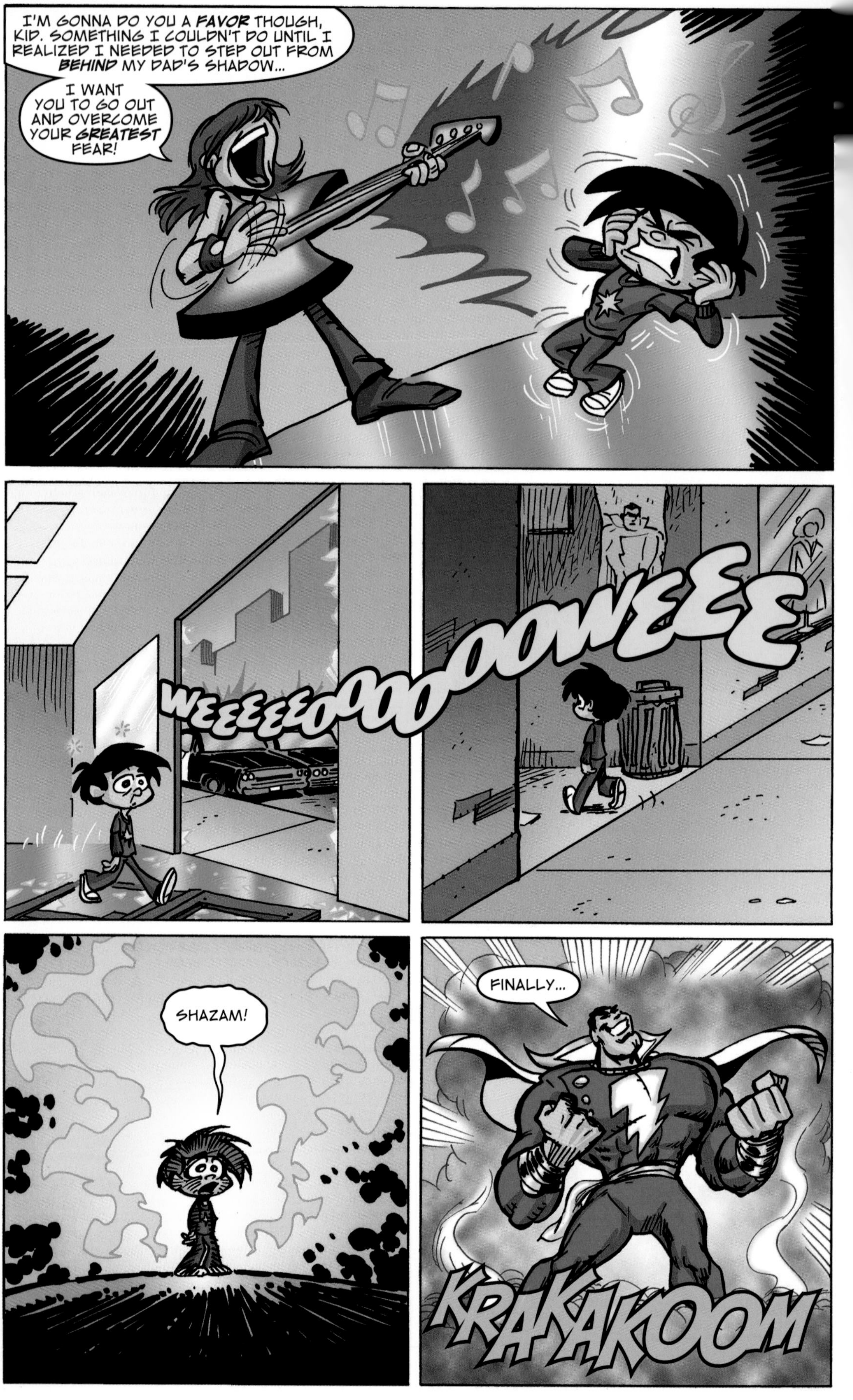

I'M GONNA DO YOU A FAVOR THOUGH, KID. SOMETHING I COULDN'T DO UNTIL I REALIZED I NEEDED TO STEP OUT FROM BEHIND MY DAD'S SHADOW...
I WANT YOU TO GO OUT AND OVERCOME YOUR GREATEST FEAR!
WEEEEEOOOOOOOWEEE
SHAZAM!
FINALLY...
KRAKAKOOM

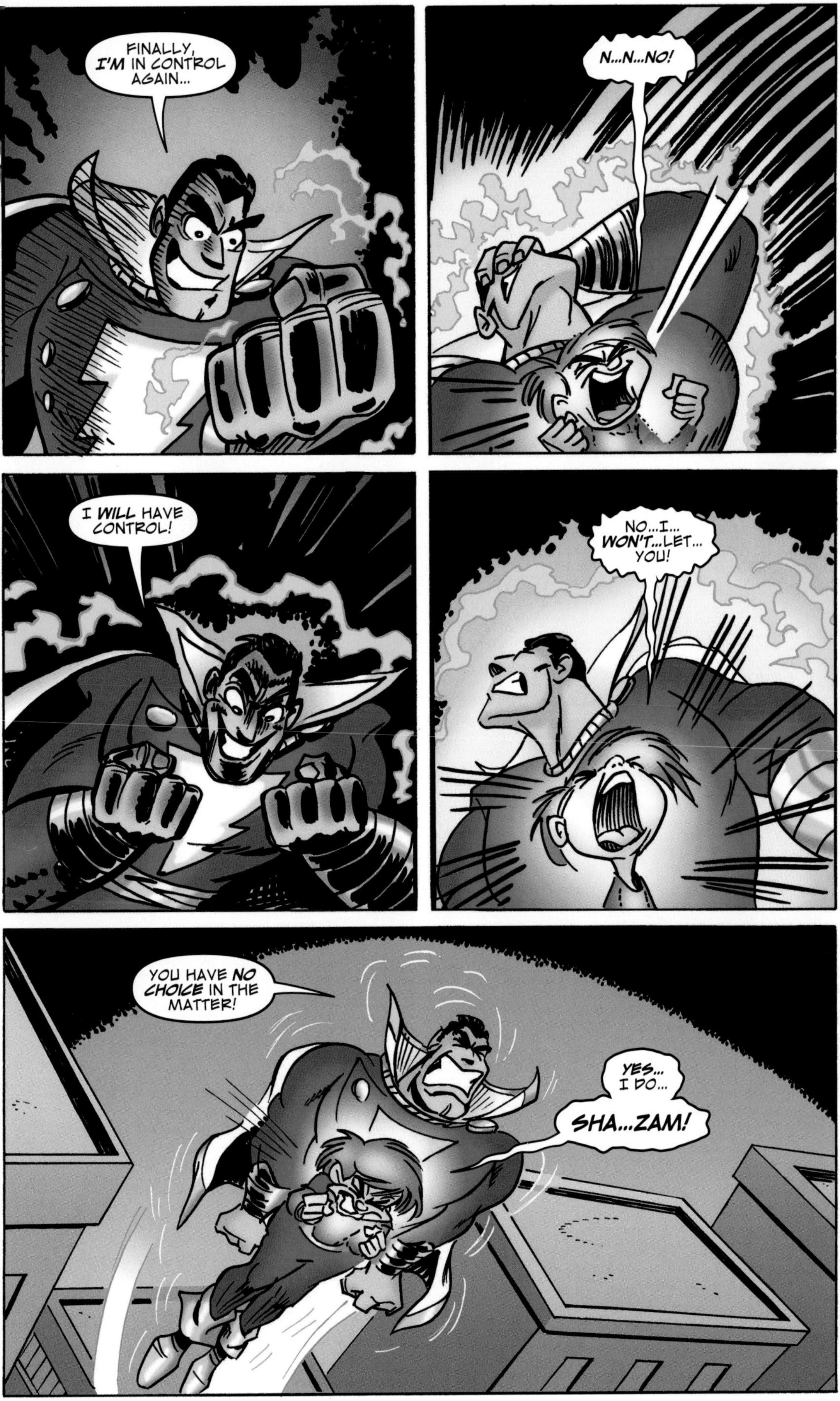
FINALLY, I'M IN CONTROL AGAIN...
N...N...NO!
I WILL HAVE CONTROL!
NO...I... WON'T...LET... YOU!
YOU HAVE NO CHOICE IN THE MATTER!
YES... I DO...
SHA...ZAM!

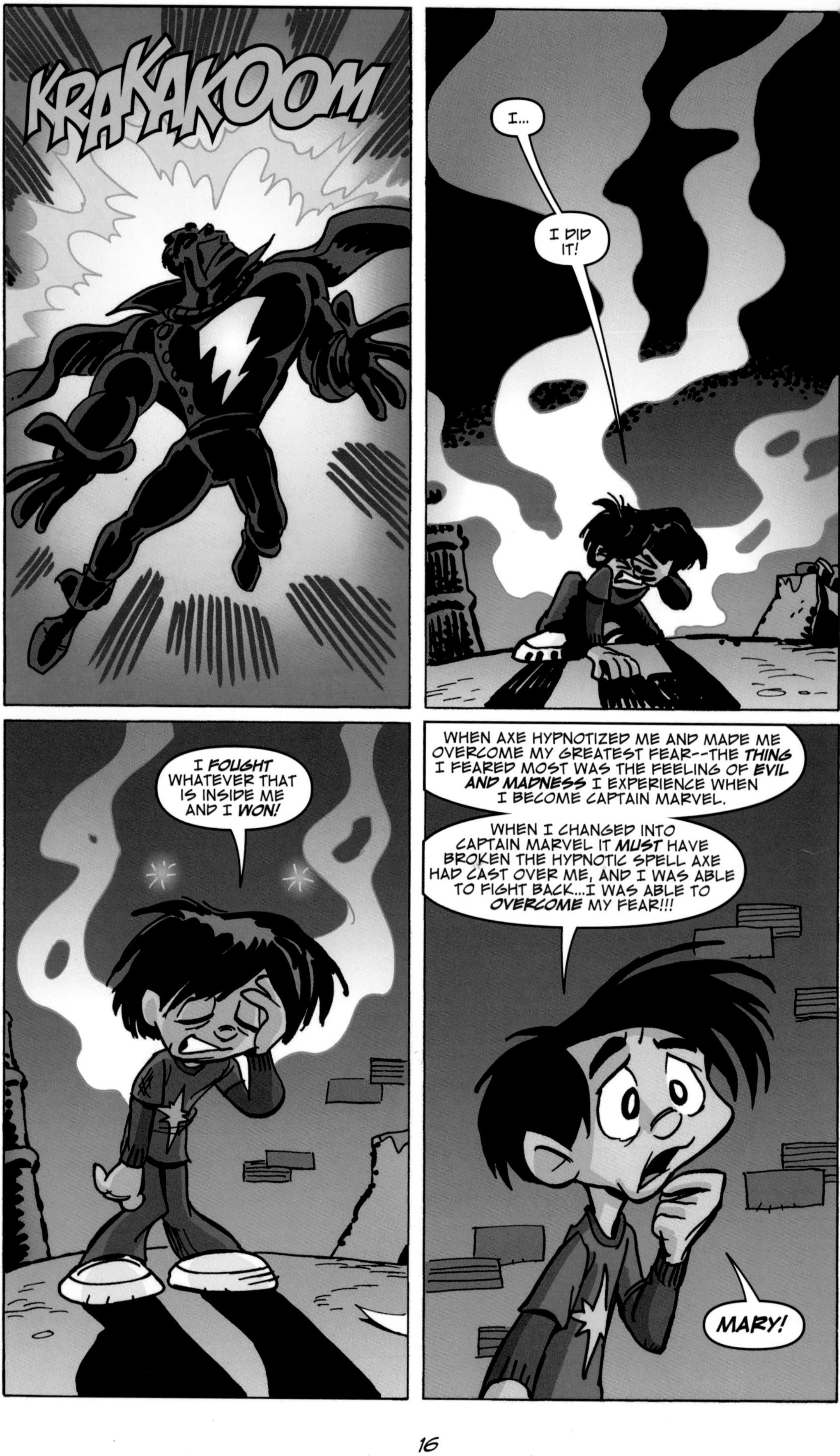

KRAKAKOOM
I...
I DID IT!
I FOUGHT WHATEVER THAT IS INSIDE ME AND I WON!
WHEN AXE HYPNOTIZED ME AND MADE ME OVERCOME MY GREATEST FEAR--THE THING I FEARED MOST WAS THE FEELING OF EVIL AND MADNESS I EXPERIENCE WHEN I BECOME CAPTAIN MARVEL.
WHEN I CHANGED INTO CAPTAIN MARVEL IT MUST HAVE BROKEN THE HYPNOTIC SPELL AXE HAD CAST OVER ME, AND I WAS ABLE TO FIGHT BACK...I WAS ABLE TO OVERCOME MY FEAR!!!
MARY!

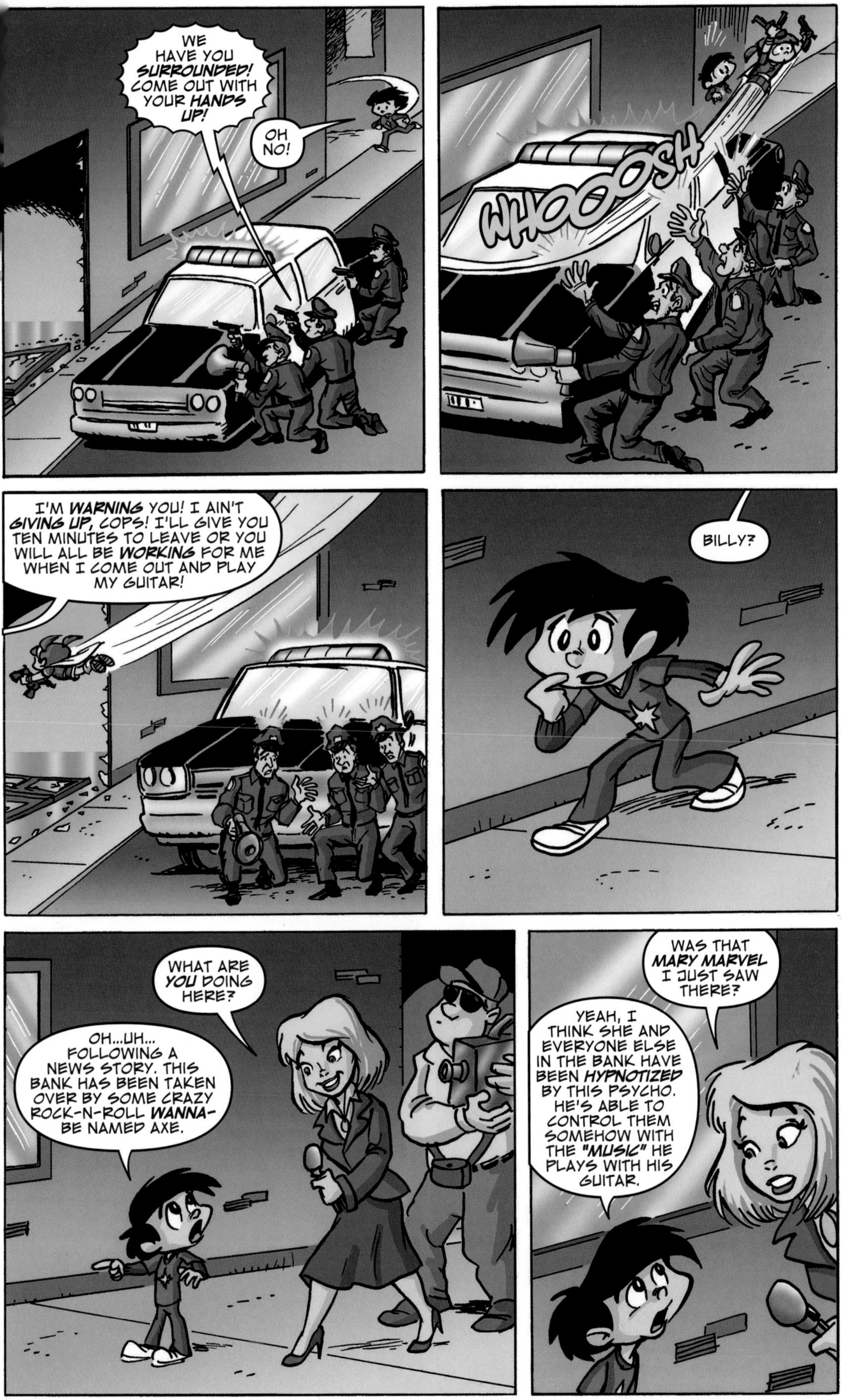
WE HAVE YOU SURROUNDED! COME OUT WITH YOUR HANDS UP!
OH NO!
WHOOOOSH
I'M WARNING YOU! I AIN'T GIVING UP, COPS! I'LL GIVE YOU TEN MINUTES TO LEAVE OR YOU WILL ALL BE WORKING FOR ME WHEN I COME OUT AND PLAY MY GUITAR!
BILLY?
WHAT ARE YOU DOING HERE?
OH...UH... FOLLOWING A NEWS STORY. THIS BANK HAS BEEN TAKEN OVER BY SOME CRAZY ROCK-N-ROLL WANNA-BE NAMED AXE.
WAS THAT MARY MARVEL I JUST SAW THERE?
YEAH, I THINK SHE AND EVERYONE ELSE IN THE BANK HAVE BEEN HYPNOTIZED BY THIS PSYCHO. HE'S ABLE TO CONTROL THEM SOMEHOW WITH THE "MUSIC" HE PLAYS WITH HIS GUITAR.

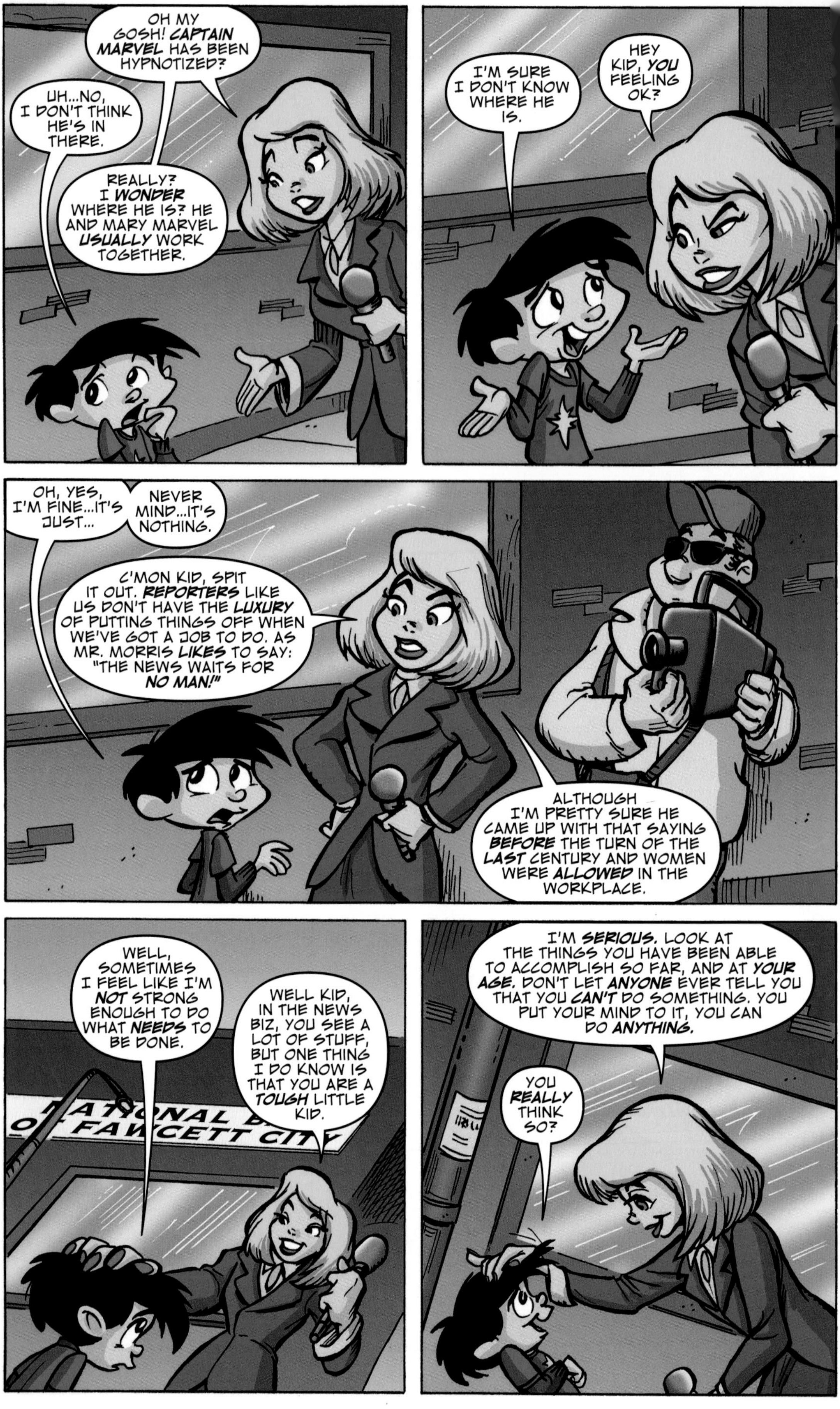
OH MY GOSH! CAPTAIN MARVEL HAS BEEN HYPNOTIZED?
UH...NO, I DON'T THINK HE'S IN THERE.
REALLY? I WONDER WHERE HE IS? HE AND MARY MARVEL USUALLY WORK TOGETHER.
I'M SURE I DON'T KNOW WHERE HE IS.
HEY KID, YOU FEELING OK?
OH, YES, I'M FINE...IT'S JUST...
NEVER MIND...IT'S NOTHING.
C'MON KID, SPIT IT OUT. REPORTERS LIKE US DON'T HAVE THE LUXURY OF PUTTING THINGS OFF WHEN WE'VE GOT A JOB TO DO. AS MR. MORRIS LIKES TO SAY: "THE NEWS WAITS FOR NO MAN!"
ALTHOUGH I'M PRETTY SURE HE CAME UP WITH THAT SAYING BEFORE THE TURN OF THE LAST CENTURY AND WOMEN WERE ALLOWED IN THE WORKPLACE.
WELL, SOMETIMES I FEEL LIKE I'M NOT STRONG ENOUGH TO DO WHAT NEEDS TO BE DONE.
WELL KID, IN THE NEWS BIZ, YOU SEE A LOT OF STUFF, BUT ONE THING I DO KNOW IS THAT YOU ARE A TOUGH LITTLE KID.
NATIONAL B... OF FAWCETT CITY
I'M SERIOUS. LOOK AT THE THINGS YOU HAVE BEEN ABLE TO ACCOMPLISH SO FAR, AND AT YOUR AGE. DON'T LET ANYONE EVER TELL YOU THAT YOU CAN'T DO SOMETHING. YOU PUT YOUR MIND TO IT, YOU CAN DO ANYTHING.
YOU REALLY THINK SO?

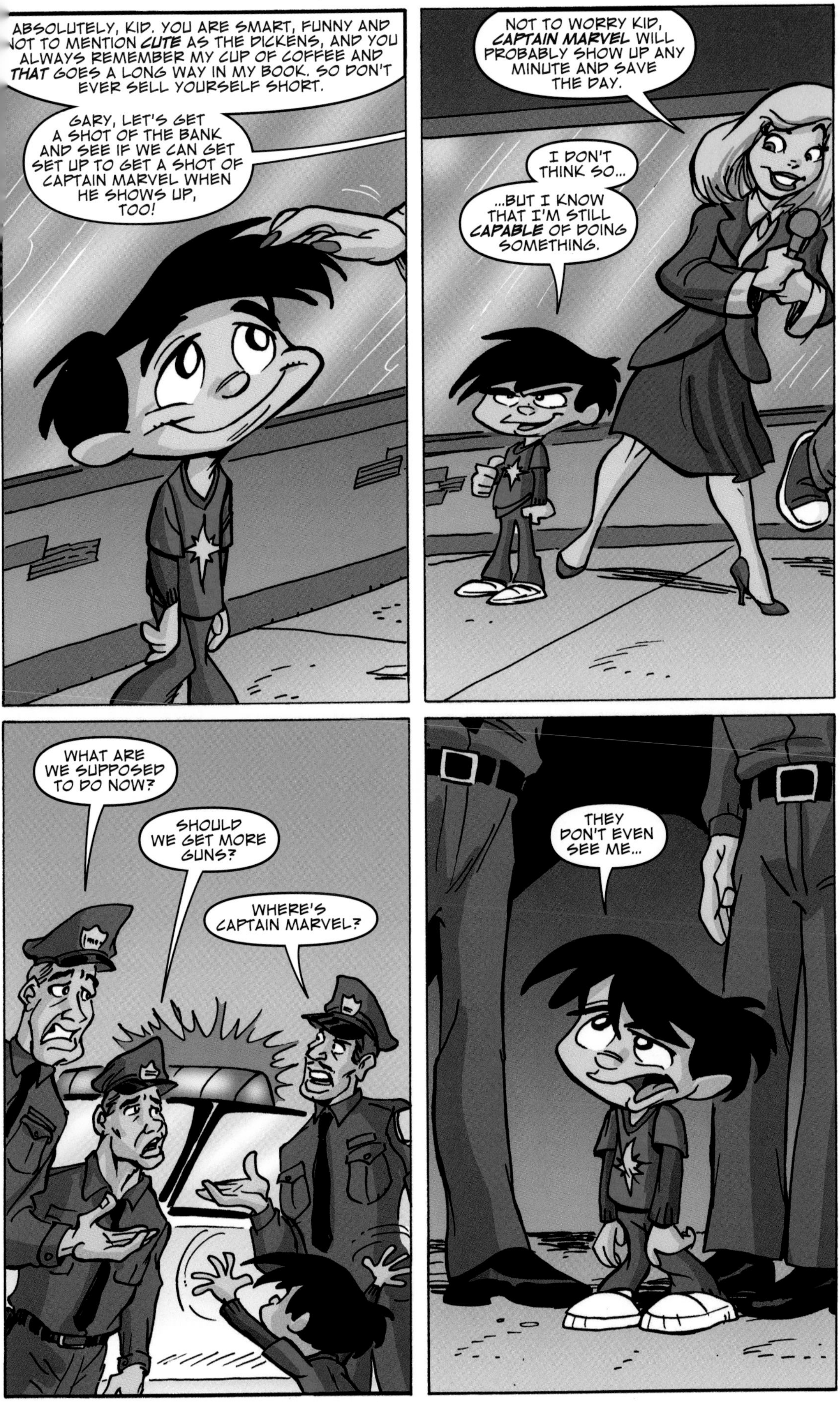
ABSOLUTELY, KID. YOU ARE SMART, FUNNY AND NOT TO MENTION CUTE AS THE DICKENS, AND YOU ALWAYS REMEMBER MY CUP OF COFFEE AND THAT GOES A LONG WAY IN MY BOOK. SO DON'T EVER SELL YOURSELF SHORT.
GARY, LET'S GET A SHOT OF THE BANK AND SEE IF WE CAN GET SET UP TO GET A SHOT OF CAPTAIN MARVEL WHEN HE SHOWS UP, TOO!
NOT TO WORRY KID, CAPTAIN MARVEL WILL PROBABLY SHOW UP ANY MINUTE AND SAVE THE DAY.
I DON'T THINK SO...
...BUT I KNOW THAT I'M STILL CAPABLE OF DOING SOMETHING.
WHAT ARE WE SUPPOSED TO DO NOW?
SHOULD WE GET MORE GUNS?
WHERE'S CAPTAIN MARVEL?
THEY DON'T EVEN SEE ME...

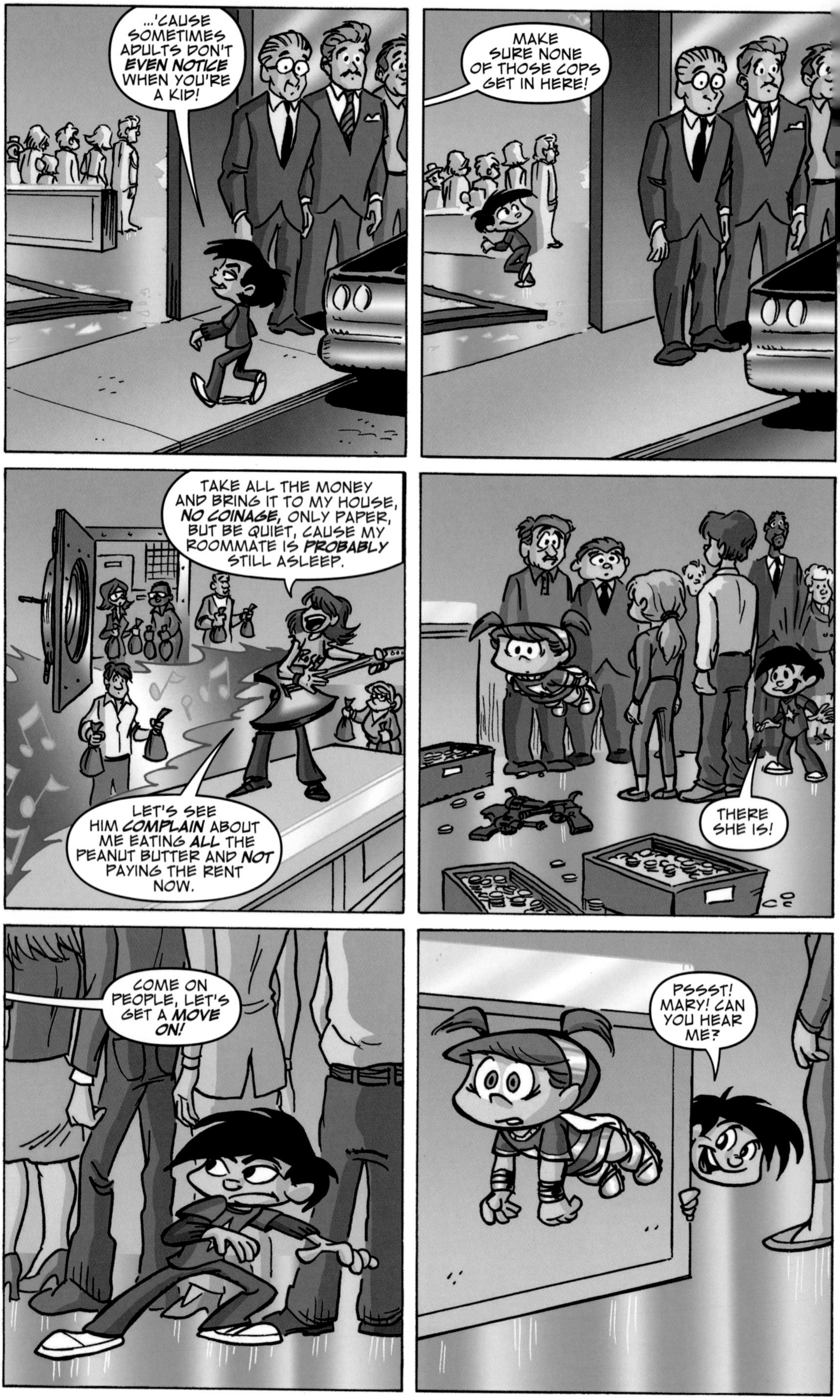
...'CAUSE SOMETIMES ADULTS DON'T EVEN NOTICE WHEN YOU'RE A KID!
MAKE SURE NONE OF THOSE COPS GET IN HERE!
TAKE ALL THE MONEY AND BRING IT TO MY HOUSE, NO COINAGE, ONLY PAPER, BUT BE QUIET, CAUSE MY ROOMMATE IS PROBABLY STILL ASLEEP.
LET'S SEE HIM COMPLAIN ABOUT ME EATING ALL THE PEANUT BUTTER AND NOT PAYING THE RENT NOW.
THERE SHE IS!
COME ON PEOPLE, LET'S GET A MOVE ON!
PSSST! MARY! CAN YOU HEAR ME?

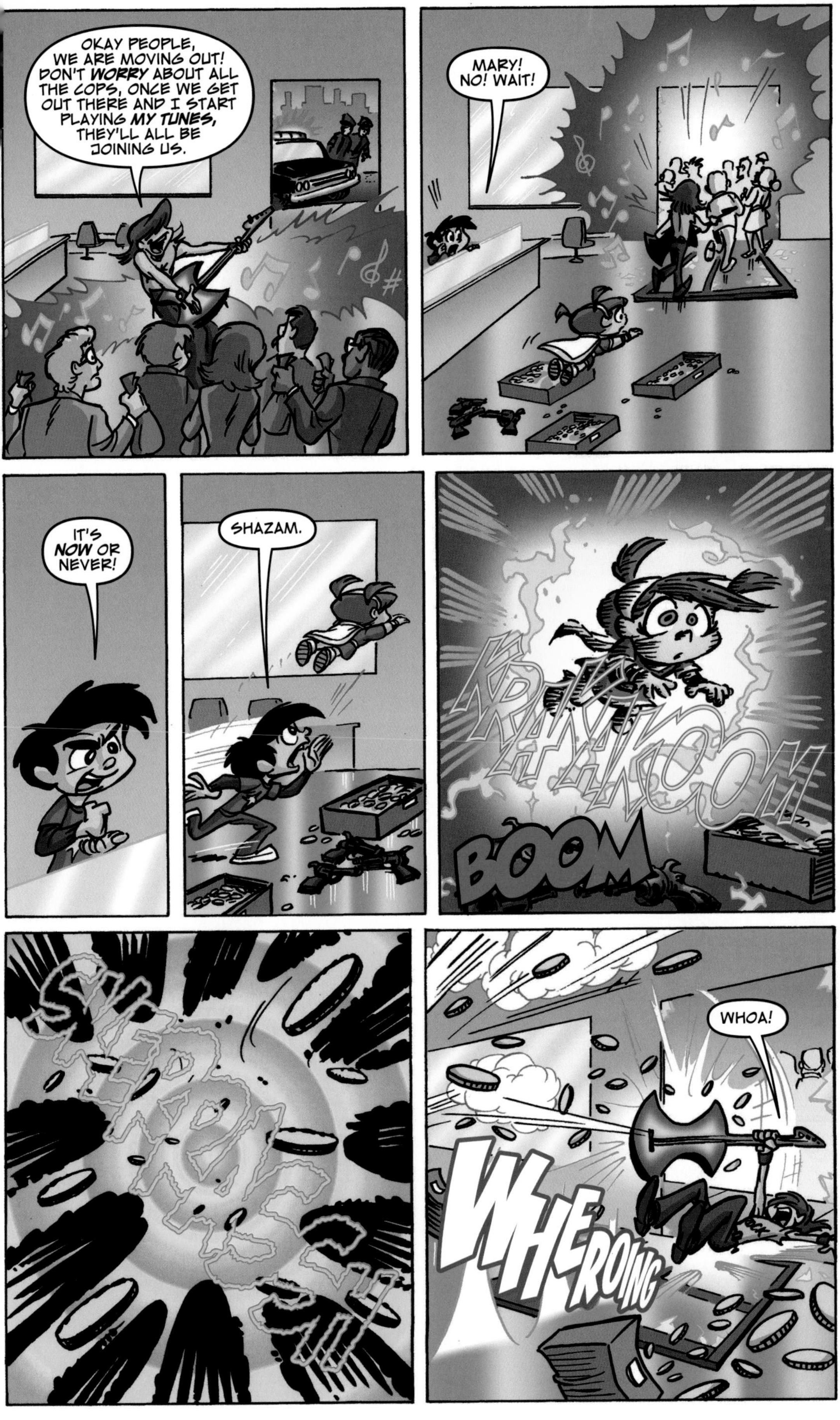
OKAY PEOPLE, WE ARE MOVING OUT! DON'T WORRY ABOUT ALL THE COPS, ONCE WE GET OUT THERE AND I START PLAYING MY TUNES, THEY'LL ALL BE JOINING US.
MARY! NO! WAIT!
IT'S NOW OR NEVER!
SHAZAM.
KRAKAKOOM
BOOM
WHOA!
WHEROING

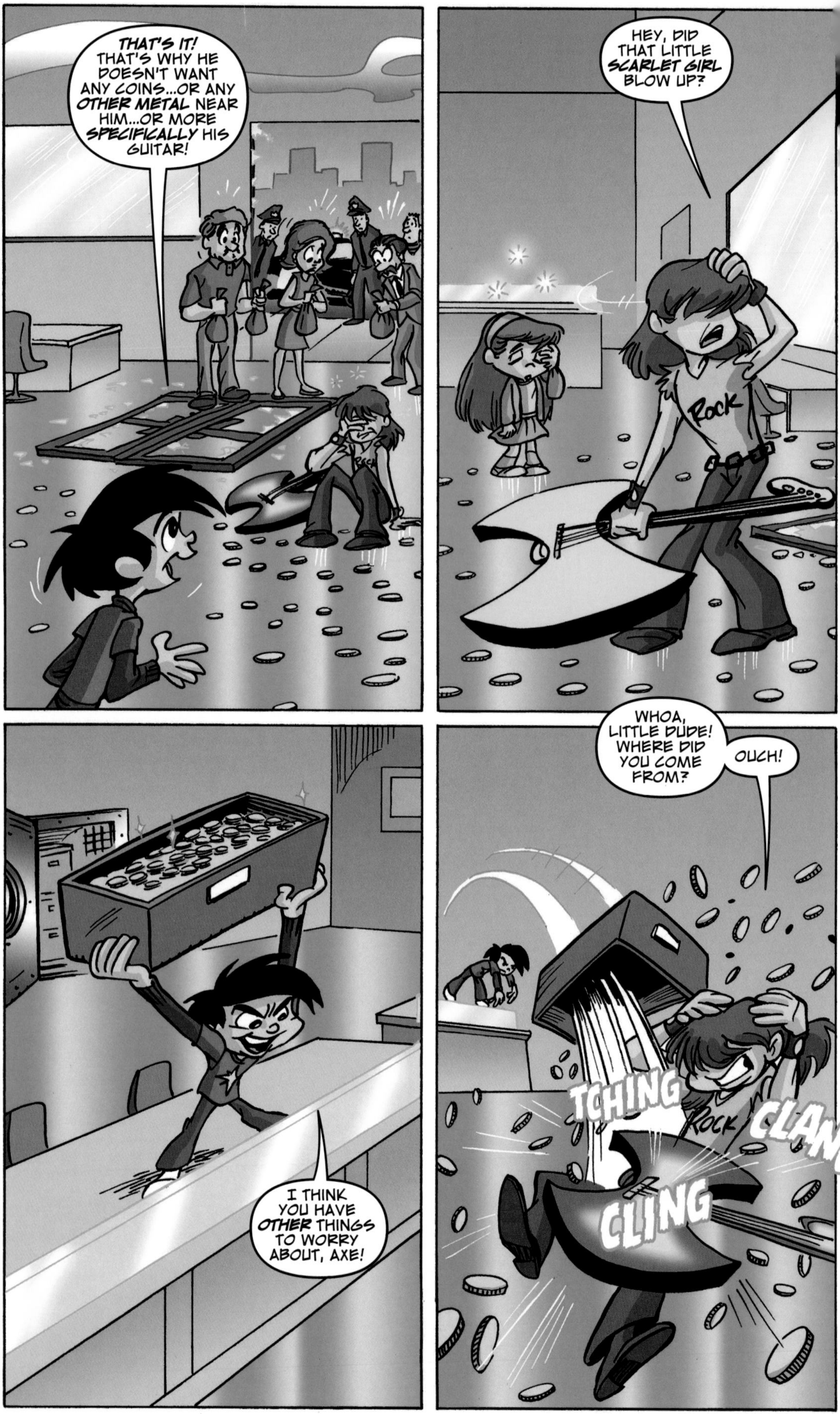
THAT'S IT! THAT'S WHY HE DOESN'T WANT ANY COINS...OR ANY OTHER METAL NEAR HIM...OR MORE SPECIFICALLY HIS GUITAR!
HEY, DID THAT LITTLE SCARLET GIRL BLOW UP?
ROCK
I THINK YOU HAVE OTHER THINGS TO WORRY ABOUT, AXE!
WHOA, LITTLE DUDE! WHERE DID YOU COME FROM?
OUCH!
TCHING
CLANG
CLING

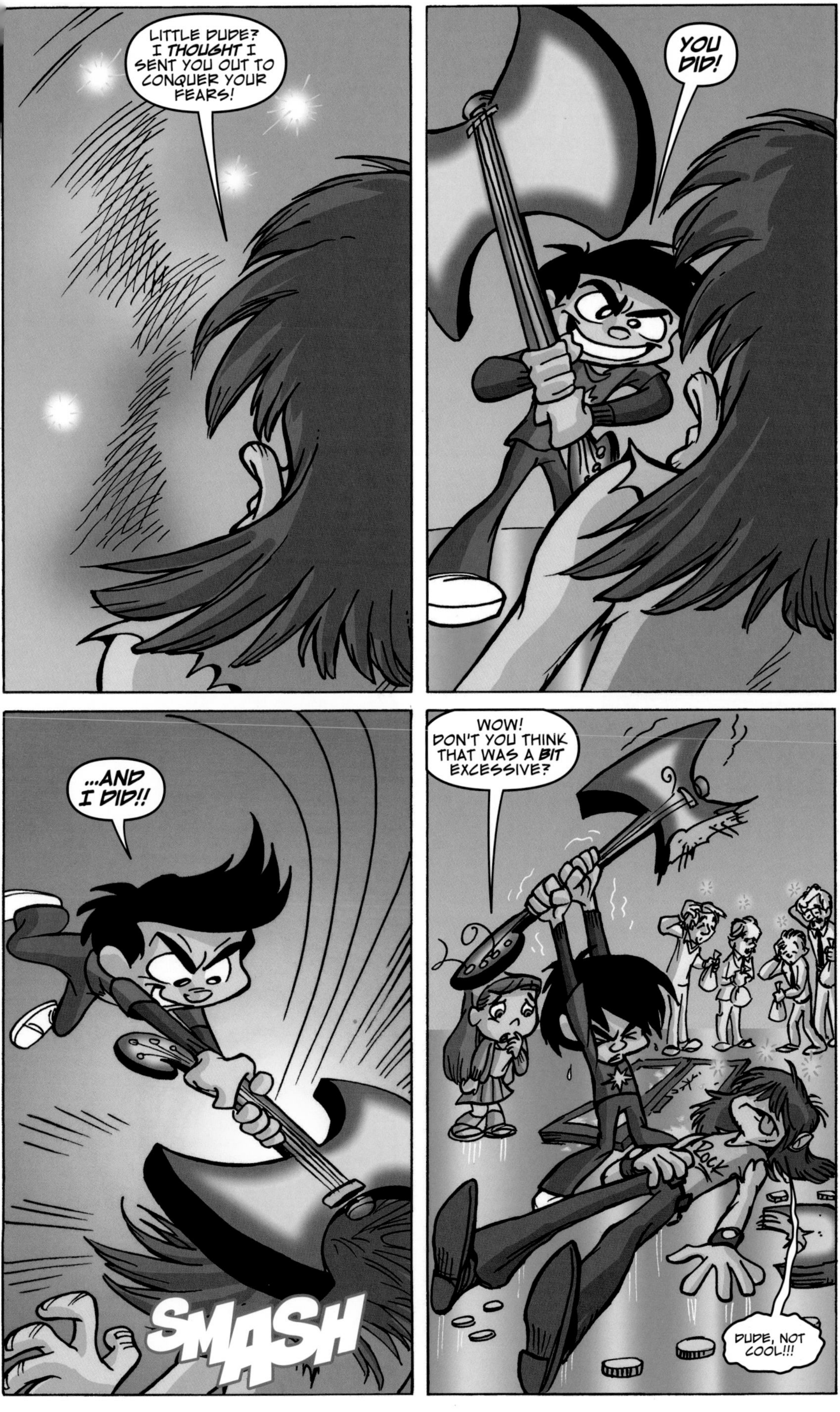

LITTLE DUDE? I THOUGHT I SENT YOU OUT TO CONQUER YOUR FEARS!
YOU DID!
...AND I DID!!
SMASH
WOW! DON'T YOU THINK THAT WAS A BIT EXCESSIVE?
ROCK
DUDE, NOT COOL!!!

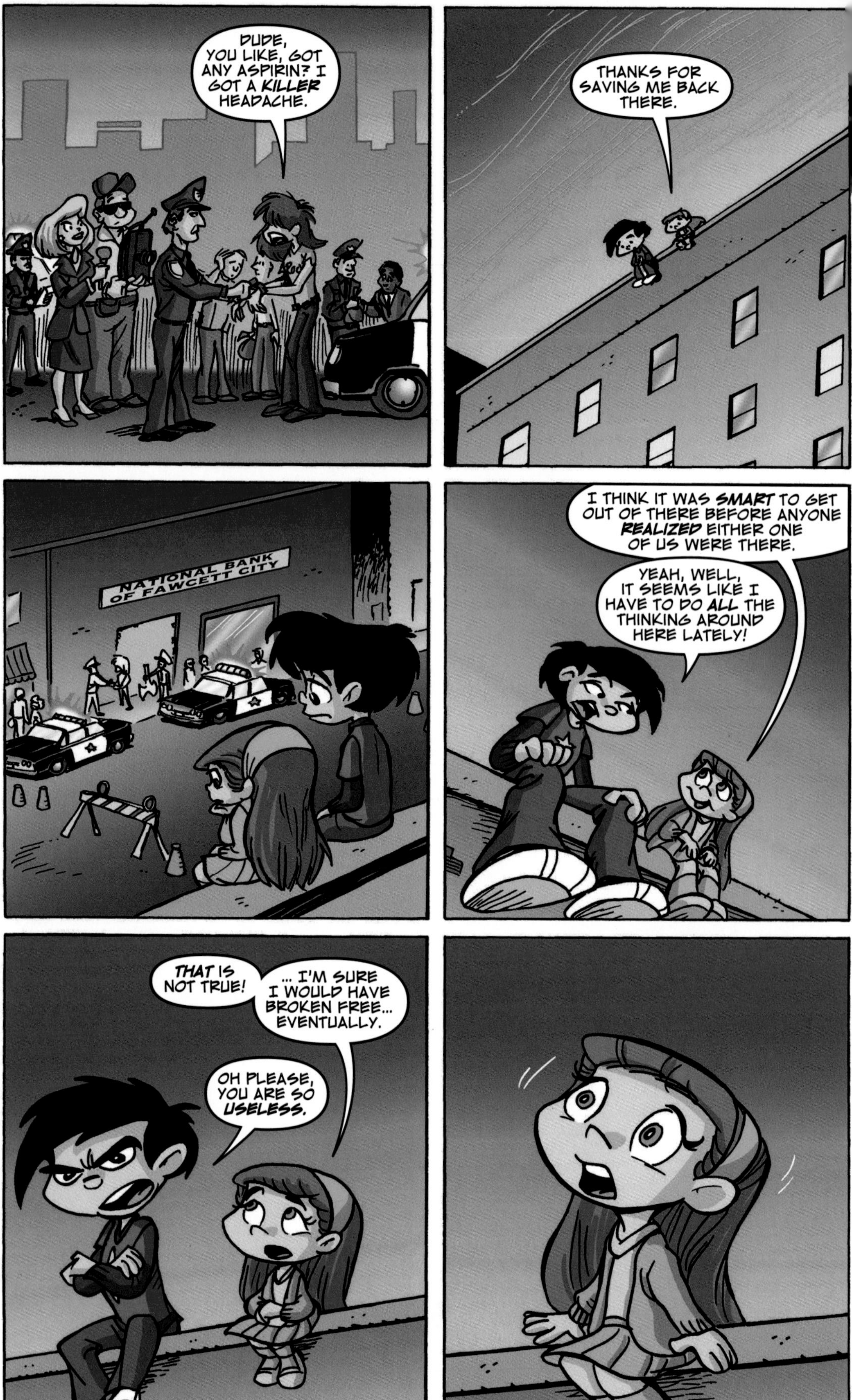
DUDE, YOU LIKE, GOT ANY ASPIRIN? I GOT A KILLER HEADACHE.
THANKS FOR SAVING ME BACK THERE.
NATIONAL BANK OF FAWCETT CITY
I THINK IT WAS SMART TO GET OUT OF THERE BEFORE ANYONE REALIZED EITHER ONE OF US WERE THERE.
YEAH, WELL, IT SEEMS LIKE I HAVE TO DO ALL THE THINKING AROUND HERE LATELY!
THAT IS NOT TRUE!
... I'M SURE I WOULD HAVE BROKEN FREE... EVENTUALLY.
OH PLEASE, YOU ARE SO USELESS.

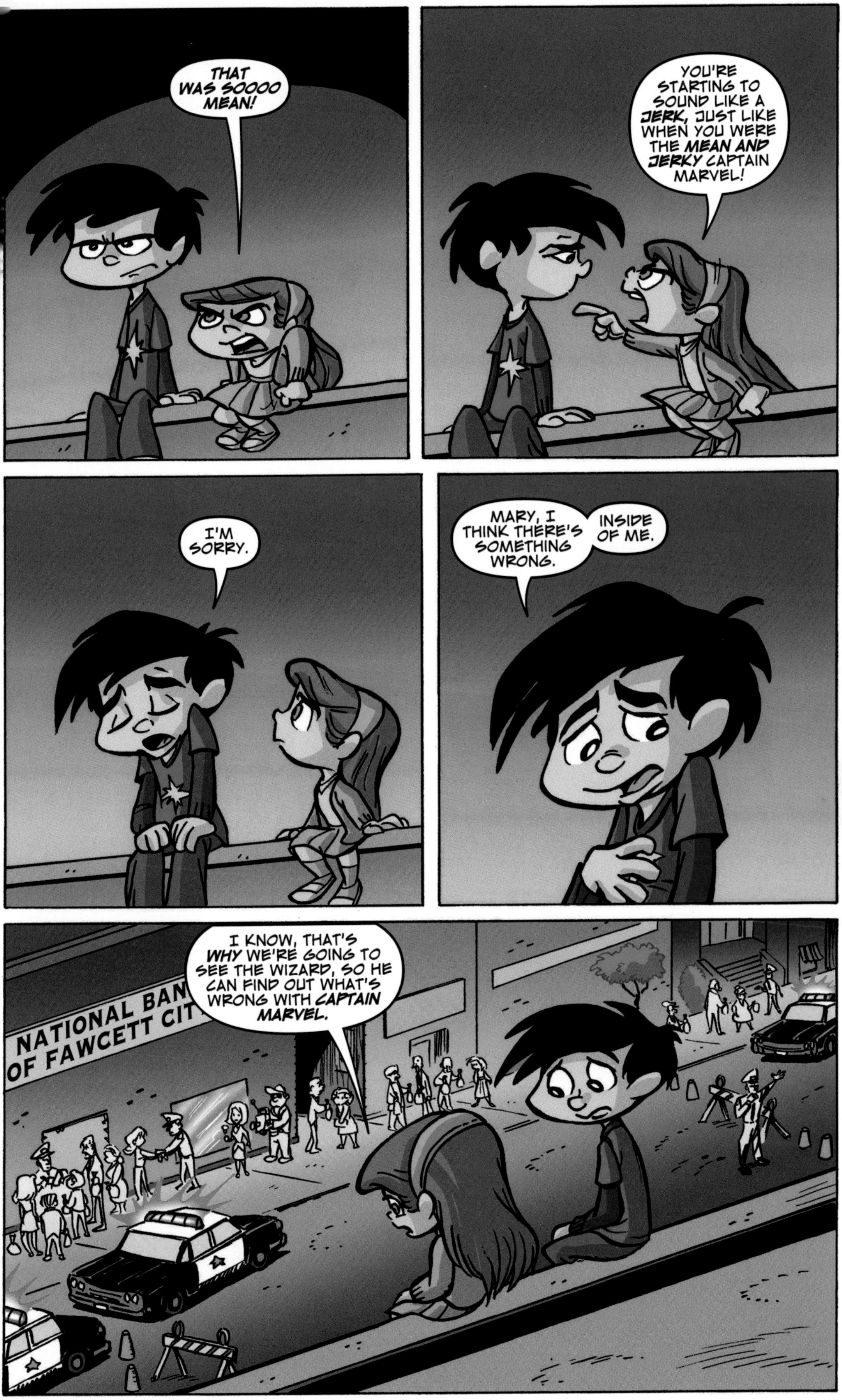
THAT WAS SOOOO MEAN!
YOU'RE STARTING TO SOUND LIKE A JERK, JUST LIKE WHEN YOU WERE THE MEAN AND JERKY CAPTAIN MARVEL!
I'M SORRY.
MARY, I THINK THERE'S SOMETHING WRONG.
INSIDE OF ME.
I KNOW, THAT'S WHY WE'RE GOING TO SEE THE WIZARD, SO HE CAN FIND OUT WHAT'S WRONG WITH CAPTAIN MARVEL.
NATIONAL BAN
OF FAWCETT CIT

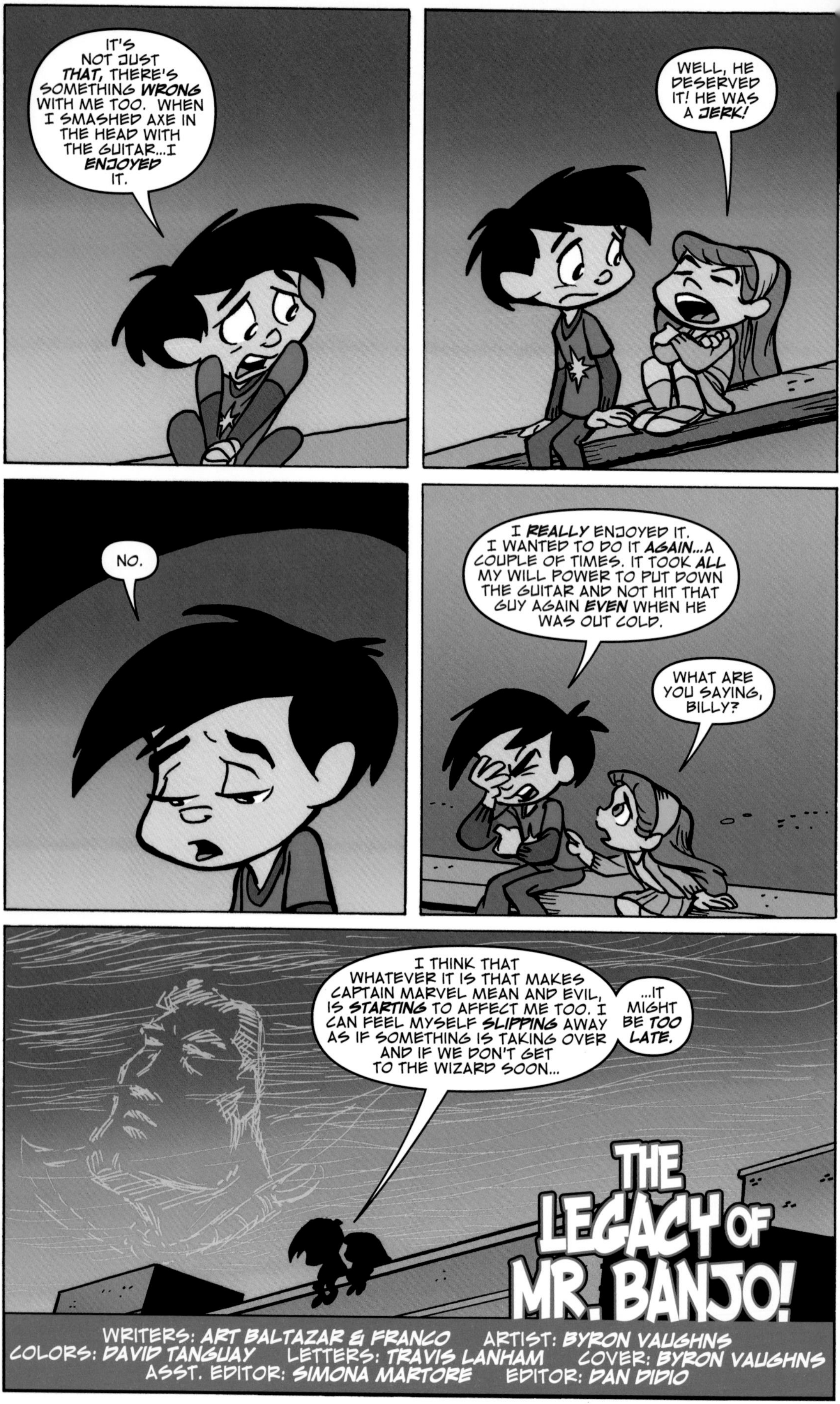

IT'S NOT JUST THAT, THERE'S SOMETHING WRONG WITH ME TOO. WHEN I SMASHED AXE IN THE HEAD WITH THE GUITAR...I ENJOYED IT.
WELL, HE DESERVED IT! HE WAS A JERK!
NO.
I REALLY ENJOYED IT. I WANTED TO DO IT AGAIN...A COUPLE OF TIMES. IT TOOK ALL MY WILL POWER TO PUT DOWN THE GUITAR AND NOT HIT THAT GUY AGAIN EVEN WHEN HE WAS OUT COLD.
WHAT ARE YOU SAYING, BILLY?
I THINK THAT WHATEVER IT IS THAT MAKES CAPTAIN MARVEL MEAN AND EVIL, IS STARTING TO AFFECT ME TOO. I CAN FEEL MYSELF SLIPPING AWAY AS IF SOMETHING IS TAKING OVER AND IF WE DON'T GET TO THE WIZARD SOON...
...IT MIGHT BE TOO LATE.
THE LEGACY OF MR. BANJO!
WRITERS: ART BALTAZAR & FRANCO ARTIST: BYRON VAUGHNS
COLORS: DAVID TANGUAY LETTERS: TRAVIS LANHAM COVER: BYRON VAUGHNS
ASST. EDITOR: SIMONA MARTORE EDITOR: DAN DIDIO

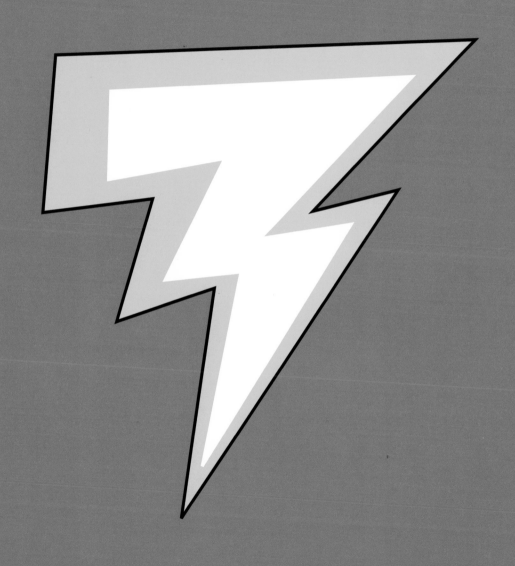

CREATORS

ART BALTAZAR - CO-WRITER

Born in Chicago, **Art Baltazar** has been cartooning ever since he can recall. Art has worked on award-winning series like Tiny Titans and Superman Family Adventures. He lives outside of Chicago with his wife, Rose, and children Sonny, Gordon, and Audrey.

FRANCO - CO-WRITER

Franco Aureliani has been drawing comics ever since he could hold a crayon. He resides in upstate New York with his wife, Ivette, and son, Nicolas, and spends most of his days working on comics. Franco has worked on Superman Family Adventures and Tiny Titans, and he also teaches high school art.

GLOSSARY

coinage (COYN-ij)--money in the form of coins

conduit (CON-doo-it)--a method of sending something one place to another

conquer (KONG-ker)--to take control of something through the use of force

dickens (DI-kenz)--a word that is used to make a statement or question more forceful

eternity (i-TER-ni-tee)--time without end

excessive (ek-SESS-siv)--over the top or too much

luxury (LUHK-shuh-ree)--something that is expensive or excessive and not necessary

monstrosity (mahn-STRAH-suh-tee)--something that is very large and ugly

portal (POHR-tuhl)--a magical gateway used for transportation

recuperating (ri-KOO-puh-ray-ting)--returning to normal health after being sick or injured

roadie (ROH-dee)--a person whose job is to help move and set up the equipment of traveling musicians

scarlet (SKAHR-lit)--a bright red color

VISUAL QUESTIONS & PROMPTS

1. What is happening in this panel? How do you know?

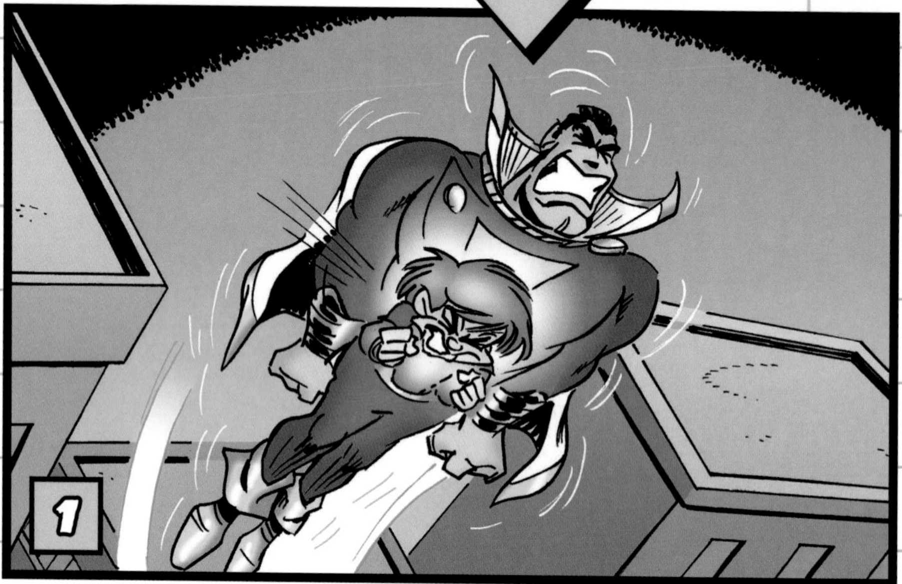

2. Why does Mary say Billy's actions are excessive in this panel? (Hint: read the definition of "excessive" in the glossary.) What do you think is happening to Billy that is making him act this way?

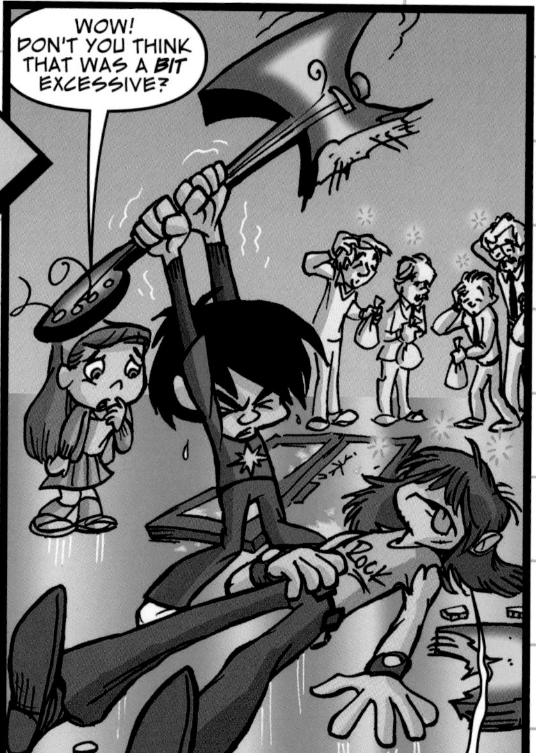
WOW! DON'T YOU THINK THAT WAS A BIT EXCESSIVE?
DUDE, NOT COOL!!!

3. Whose face do we see in the wind? Why do you think the artist put it there?

4. What do the waves coming from this guitar mean? How do they affect Mary?

READ THEM ALL!

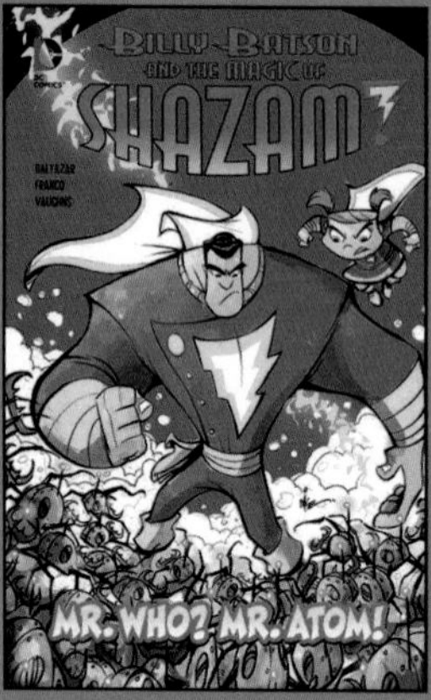
BILLY BATSON AND THE MAGIC OF SHAZAM!
BALTAZAR
FRANCO
VAUGHNS
MR. WHO? MR. ATOM!

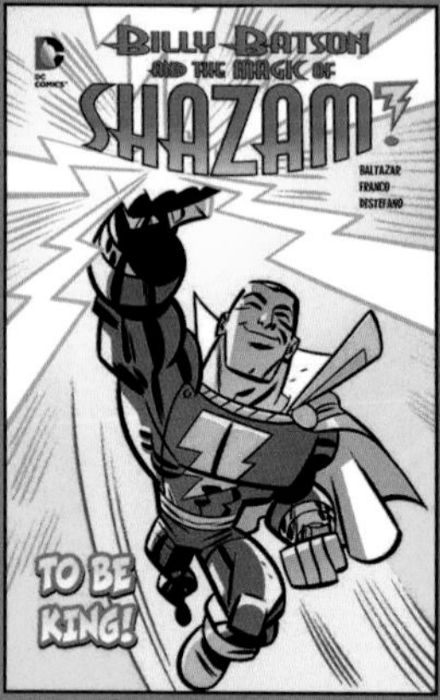
BILLY BATSON AND THE MAGIC OF SHAZAM!
BALTAZAR
FRANCO
DESTEFANO
TO BE KING!

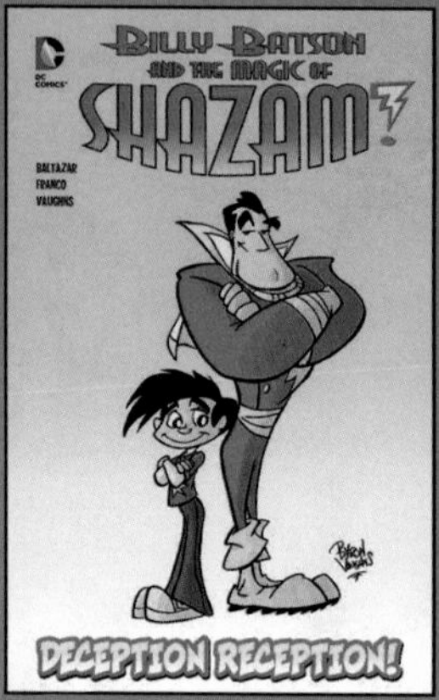
BILLY BATSON AND THE MAGIC OF SHAZAM!
BALTAZAR
FRANCO
VAUGHNS
DECEPTION RECEPTION!

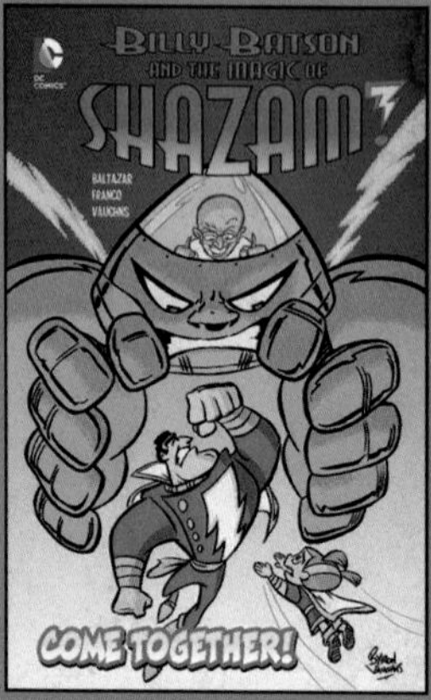
BILLY BATSON AND THE MAGIC OF SHAZAM!
BALTAZAR
FRANCO
VAUGHNS
COME TOGETHER!

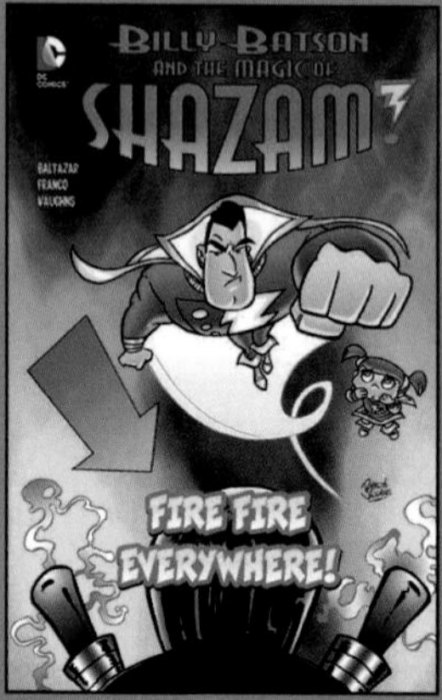
BILLY BATSON AND THE MAGIC OF SHAZAM!
BALTAZAR
FRANCO
VAUGHNS
FIRE FIRE EVERYWHERE!

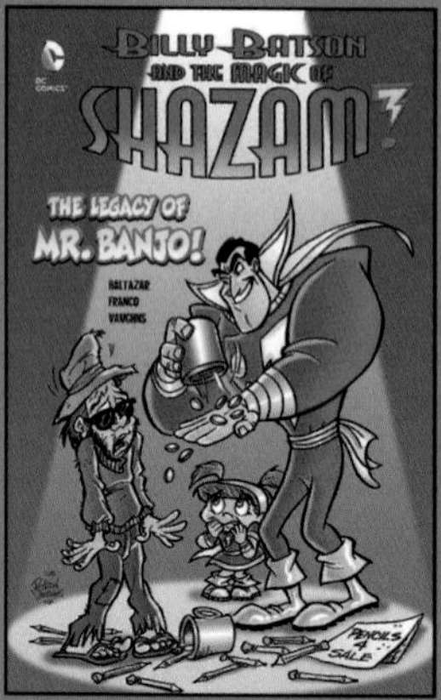
BILLY BATSON AND THE MAGIC OF SHAZAM!
THE LEGACY OF MR. BANJO!
BALTAZAR
FRANCO
VAUGHNS

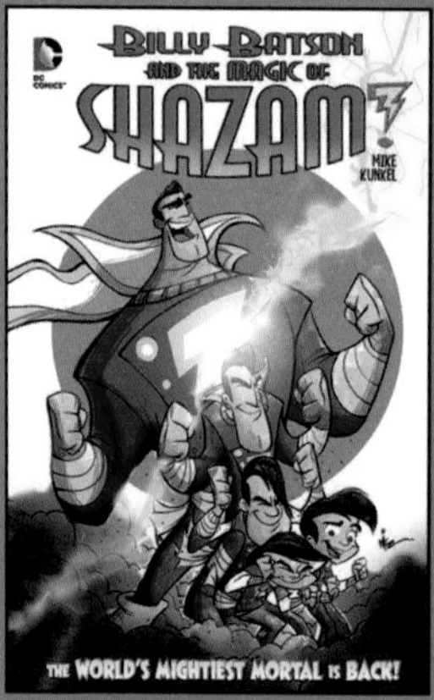
BILLY BATSON AND THE MAGIC OF SHAZAM!
MIKE KUNKEL
THE WORLD'S MIGHTIEST MORTAL IS BACK!

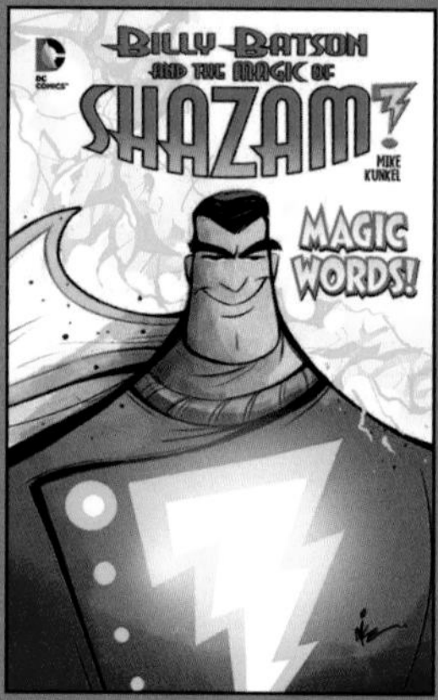
BILLY BATSON AND THE MAGIC OF SHAZAM!
MIKE KUNKEL
MAGIC WORDS!

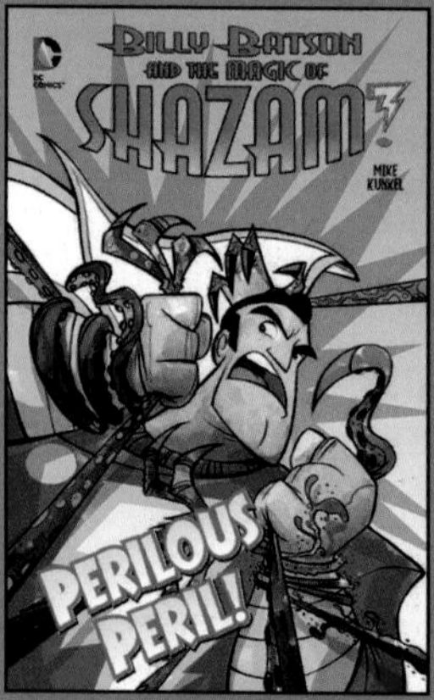
BILLY BATSON AND THE MAGIC OF SHAZAM!
MIKE KUNKEL
PERILOUS PERIL!

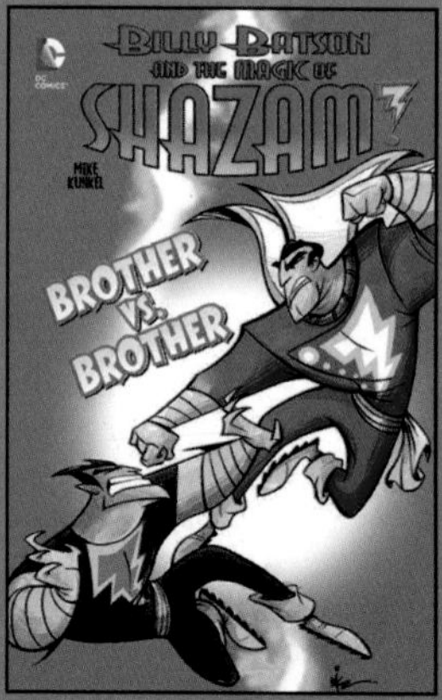
BILLY BATSON AND THE MAGIC OF SHAZAM!
MIKE KUNKEL
BROTHER VS. BROTHER